I0517321

Marge Simon: 27, 49, and 68
Chris Friend: pages 2, 37, 73, 85, and 86
Sandy DeLuca: front cover and pages 4, 12, 42, 50, 53, and 79
Elizabeth Hattie Pierce-Collins: pages 17, 48, 75, 81, and 90
Denny E. Marshall: back cover and pages 10, 32, and 62
Lonnie Weems: page 25

Night to Dawn No. 43, April, 2023, Copyright 2023 by Barbara Custer. All rights revert to individual author and artist after publication. ISSN # 1542-1430; ISBN: 978-1-937769-78-9

Night to Dawn is a semi-annual publication of fiction, poetry, artwork, articles, and review.

Orders, editorial, and queries: Barbara Custer, P. O. Box 643, Abington, PA 19001

Email: barbaracuster@hotmail.com or ntdsubmissions@gmail.com

PayPal orders: venus1021@juno.com.

Submissions: ntdsubmissions@gmail.com; Web: www.bloodredshadow.com

FREE Vampires, werewolves, and zombies oh my! Chris Friend, Apt # 608, Market Manor, 1030 Market St. Parkersburg, West Virginia 26101. Send self-addressed, stamped envelope for free copies of my Mars newsletter.

Pickings and Tidbits

Top of the balloon to you! 😊

I'm focusing on spring weather, as I'm not too fond of winter weather. Many people feel the same way unless they're into winter sports. No trick n' treaters came this past Halloween because, I guess, it was raining and cold. We didn't let foul weather stop us in my childhood, but times have changed. November was milder than October—at least part of it.

Night to Dawn 43 offers a unique take on monsters. One of them is a Mylar balloon. Dat's wight, wabbits, an author crafted a horror tale about an evil balloon that takes on a life of its own and attacks the protag. Enter Katherine Quevedo's story, "Hell-ium Balloon."

Most tales feature the walking dead as monsters seeking out human flesh. But Anna Rose's "The Forest" features a walking dead man who befriends a lost child and becomes a hero. Waiting for a train is a mundane chore, but in Marge Simon's "Waiting," the trains pass a hapless would-be rider by, leaving her victim to the ravages of vampires who haunt the station. Two young brothers visit their late daddy's grave, singing the family's favorite song in Ken Goldman's "Hokey Pokey," disturbing their father's eternal rest.

Lee Clark Zumpe contributed some spooky material. My favorite was "Manor of Madness," featuring an amusement ride that takes passengers to an alternate dimension where terrible things happen. The Philadelphia State Hospital at Byberry (closed 1990) was labored "Philadelphia's House of Horrors," but Linda Barrett takes the horrors to a new level in "Mike Walker in Byberry." In Rod Marsden's "Great Adventure," a young couple discovers love, but not in the usual way. Christopher T. Dabrowski's two short tales start in the real world, but the end packs a punch with self-inflicted burns and stairs leading to Heaven.

Everyone hates inflation, but some characters in Hal Kempka's tale, "Free Trade," handle it by resorting to cannibalism. Beware of Hilary Lyons' "Soporific Pillows of Pan." These pillows will lure you into a hostile universe inhabited by beings that thirst for blood. In addition to her art on the front cover and interior pages, Sandy DeLuca sent two short stories. The first, "Girls on the Road," reminded me of the *Thelma and Louise* movie, except this story involves bloodletting. The second, "Treasure," ended sadly, and I felt bad for the narrator. Rajeev Bhargava's "Yōkai" starts as a quiet evening between a husband and his wife and ends with her having him for dinner.

Artist Lonnie Weems managed to work on another illustration featured in this issue. Marge Simon contributed delightful poetry and art to go with her short stories with the vampire theme. There will be more literary work from Marge Simon and Sandy DeLuca in the next issue. Denny E. Marshall contributed back cover art, interior illustrations, and poetry; Elizabeth Hattie Pierce and Chris Friend also contributed interior illustrations. Chris Friend is also doing a newsletter called *Mars*, as noted in his ad.

With each story in this issue, look for haunting poetry from Lee Clark Zumpe, Alexis Child, Marge Simon, Matthew Wilson, Denny E. Marshall, and Todd Hanks.

Kevin R. Doyle's *The Anchor* went live in November. A teacher once asked the class, "What will you do to achieve success?" In *The Anchor*, a young man with a crush on a newscaster offs the competition on her job, or so it seems. Does the plan work? Read the book and find out. It's available online through Amazon and other retailers. This coming year I have in mind to publish more books, and I'm hoping to finish my WIP.

In the meantime, I'm hibernating, except when I go to the food bank and senior center to volunteer. Everyone needs a balloon, even if it's not a balloon I'm providing, especially when they're sick or down on their luck. This winter is turning out to be brutally cold. Aside from that, strange beings prowl the streets at night. You know, werewolves, bears, and other critters that bite. I thank the authors, poets, and illustrators for sending me their work and the readers who enjoy the magazine. I appreciate any attention given to my work. ~~*Barbara of the Balloons*

Conversion
by
Lee Clark Zumpe

"Don't be stupid, Alex." Rose glared at Alex for a moment, the anger in her eyes making him feel impotent. So it had come to this. She could denigrate him with a mere glance. Finally, she spun around on her heels and marched down the darkened alley, mumbling, "Of all the whores in this town, he had to go and pick me..."

Good old self-deprecating Rose, always knew how to push Alex's buttons.

He watched as the darkness swallowed her. Though she had made it clear repeatedly that she found him repulsive, he still found himself inexplicably attracted to her. His kith and kin knew little about the mortal sentiment of affection, yet he had heard himself speak of love in their most intimate moments.

He felt like a fool. Though Rose mocked and taunted him, he still found her the most beautiful and captivating woman he had ever met.

The click of her heels on the pavement echoed down the alley and drew Alex from his reflections.

"Rose! Wait!" He shot a glance up and down the sidewalk. At 2:00 a.m. in New York City, even the homeless and the addicts shunned the streets of this shadowy neighborhood. The cops routinely avoided this block, even in daylight. Hell, even the pimps and the pushers rarely trespassed here. "Wait for me; it's not safe!"

"Yeah, right."

"You don't understand," Alex shouted. He finally summoned the energy and courage to peel himself from the glow of the streetlamp and dove into the darkness. The alley stank of garbage and urine. Flies momentarily deserted scraps of rotting meat as he raced by the trash heaps. Rats scampered deeper into the mounds of rubbish. "He doesn't like to be bothered."

"I don't intend to bother him," Rose said. "I intend to do him a favor or two."

"He's not like that, Rose,"

"You don't get anywhere in this world unless you show the people in power what you are capable of..." Rose stopped in front of a doorway. A faceplate on the door read No. 145 and a store-bought sign proclaimed in big red letters NO TRESPASSING. "Is this it, then?"

"Yes, but," Alex said, staggering over his words. He waved his hands frantically. "You can't, Rose; you just can't..."

"Bull," she said. Rose took a moment to inspect herself. She wore an expensive pair of black high heels and matching stockings. Her short, red leather skirt seemed cut for a five-year-old. Her denim jacket remained unbuttoned, and she wore nothing beneath it but a pink bra. Rummaging through her purse, she pulled out some lipstick and a compact. She started to open the compact but caught herself. Instead, she smiled and threw it back into the purse, mumbling, "Guess I won't need that..."

"You aren't even listening to me," Alex fumed. He paced up and down outside No. 145, shaking his head. "Why must you insist on pursuing this any further?"

"I'm not satisfied," she said, her voice cold and harsh.

"I've given you everything."

"Not enough," she shrugged as she pounded on the door. "I want more."

A moment later, the door swung open. The man inside must have been eight feet tall. Shadows masked his face, and he wore a loose-fitting robe, making it difficult to determine his shape. He stood silently and completely still.

"Hello?" Rose said tentatively. She thrust out an arm to shake the man's hand, but he failed to respond. "I'm here to see, uh," she stuttered. "I'm here, uh, I'm here with Alex."

Alex stepped forward hesitantly, wrapping his arm around Rose. She flinched involuntarily, then snuggled into him in a spurious attempt to seem loving.

"Would you tell him I've brought a guest, Dimitri?"

The giant nodded and waved his hand to welcome the two visitors into the lobby. As they stepped from the alley into the building, the temperature dropped 20 degrees. Rose shivered, found herself drawn to Alex for warmth. She wrapped her arms around him, and he complied.

Scattered about the small lobby, Rose counted three black recliners and a loveseat scattered about the small lobby. No pictures adorned the walls. A simple red throw rug strained to cover the dingy floor. Light diffused from a parlor lamp sitting atop a coffee table.

They waited endlessly. Neither of them carried a watch. Each second lasted hours, each minute years. Rose grew restless in the company of Alex, and she fidgeted with the straps of her purse. She felt the hunger in her belly, her mouth dry up, and her lips shrivel. She prayed that she would have ample time to feed after the engagement.

Maybe tonight she could make her own kill, or at least, maybe tonight, the one Alex referred to as the Elder would provide her with her sustenance.

Alex had treated her well – Rose could not deny that fact. Since her conversion, he had been at her side each night when she awoke and each morning when she yielded to sleep. He had shared his most intimate secrets, and explained all the enigmas associated with the condition.

And he had brought her fresh blood, the fluid she needed to ensure her immortality. She had taken to it immediately, reveling in the taste and the way it warmed her belly.

She loved him, in a way. As a mentor, a father figure – not as a lover. Sex which had once been heated and feral grew cold and docile. He could not hope to fulfill her desires. That was why she sought the Elder.

"What's keeping him?" Rose broke the silence, the mixture of apprehension and thirst driving her mad.

"We'll be fortunate if he sees us at all," Alex said, rubbing his eyes. "This goes against tradition,"

"Screw tradition." Rose had never been bound by custom or a sense of decorum. "Never had time for etiquette. Way too late for me to pick up good manners now."

Just then, an ominous little man rolled into the room in an electric wheelchair. His wrinkled, ashen skin glowed in the dim glow of the parlor lamp for an instant, but then the light abandoned him altogether. It seemed that the shadows from the hallway beyond refused to release him.

"What is the meaning of this, Alex?" He spoke forcefully, and Rose trembled. That such a feeble, diminutive man could product so strong a tone could frightened her.

"She insisted, sir ... I," Alex stuttered, walked toward the man, and knelt at his side. "I couldn't stop her."

"That's always the way with you, isn't it?" He scowled at Alex, his face twisting hideously. "A little boy that can't care for his pets," he sneered, eyeing Rose. Looking back at Alex groveling beside him, he added, "You disappoint me so."

"I know. I'm sorry."

"Another vampire I suppose," he snarled, edging further into the room. The lamp sputtered and died, and shadows lurched in to claim new territory. A faint blue glow emanated from the walls, just contributing enough light for Rose to see the grotesquely petite man reach out to touch her. "Immortal, are you dear?"

"Yes," she said with a trace of pride. She took his tiny hand into her own and, stooping forward, brought it to her lips. His cold flesh shivered beneath her kiss. "Alex converted me weeks ago."

"Still using that old ruse, Alex," the old man laughed, jerking his hand away from the girl. "Not very innovative, are you?"

"No, sir," Alex mumbled. "Sorry."

"Sir, I'm not sure," Rose began, but the old man kicked her in the shin from his wheelchair.

"Quiet," he yelled, "I'll not have you speaking out of turn. If I know Alex, he made me out to be some ancient vampire patriarch whose blood-sucking neophytes control half the world from their coffins – so pay me the respect I deserve!"

Rose fell to her knees and bowed her head.

"She's got spirit for a human," he smiled at Alex. "I must say I admire your choice. Have you impregnated her?"

"I haven't had the opportunity ... my cycle was interrupted by the recent solar activity."

"'Your cycle has been WHAT?" The old man stretched, his arm extending further than should have been anatomically possible, and back-handed his partisan fiercely. "You sound like those nerveless reformists back in the Nor'Bedlha colony. You've had ample time to lay your eggs. They should be ready to hatch by now."

"I'm sorry," Alex whimpered.

"Leave her to me," he said, growling. "I'll finish the job." He glared at Rose, trembling on the floor. She had been unable to follow the conversation. She still believed that Alex had turned her into a vampire, that she would live forever. "Yes, this will be amusing."

"But what about me?" Alex asked despondently. "She was to be mine."

"You moved too slowly. Go find yourself a new mate," the old man said. "And try something different. Reshape yourself – become a dominatrix or something."

Alex stood, frowning and feeling discarded. He looked at Rose one last time and smiled. He dawdled a minute longer before backing out of the room altogether, leaving the Elder alone with the woman.

"Well, Rose," the old man said, easing back into his wheelchair, "What brought you here to me?"

"I wanted to, uh, make your acquaintance," she said, stammering. "I wanted to get to know you, your worship."

"Liar!" The Elder leaned forward, put his hand beneath the woman's chin, and lifted her head. He gazed deeply into her eyes. "You came here to sleep with me, didn't you?"

"Uh," Rose stared at the shriveled old bag of bones, his knotted fingers, and his puffy lips. "I just wanted..."

As Rose watched, the old man transformed. His flesh bulged and rippled. His round face grew longer and more solid. His pudgy body swelled and reshaped itself. In instants, the wasted old man had become a young, muscular athlete whose brawny arms robust chest, and flawless features reminded Rose of a classical Greek god.

The Elder stood and kicked the wheelchair aside. He swept Rose up into his arms and kissed her.

"Do you find me more appealing in this form?" he asked.

Rose said nothing, but her expression betrayed her passion.

"Alex said you were not interested in women."

"Alex," the Elder said as he carried her up a shadowed stairwell, "was not completely honest with you."

"Then, you aren't a vampire?" Rose grew stiff in his arms, enraged that she had been duped.

"Rose, darling, I am a powerful man. Isn't that all that matters?" The Elder looked at the woman in his arms and read her indecision. Seeing this, he captured her attention, his hypnotic eyes entrancing her. The corners of his mouth peeled back, revealing long sharp fangs.

Rose smiled, eager to be taken by another vampire.

"You want me, don't you?" The Elder gently laid her on his bed.

"Yes..." Rose answered.

The Elder needed no further consent. The mate acquiesced, and he claimed her. The corners of his mouth retracted further, and in seconds, the flesh on his face had receded, leaving a hideous, slimy stump. A single eye supported by a thick tangle of glistening sinews poked through the tissue and flitted about, studying its victim. A gaping chasm ringed by rows of jagged little teeth opened in his chest. Rose felt its stale, hot breath wash over her.

"What's the matter, Rose? Not what you expected?"

When its arms became tentacles and its forked tongue slithered over her legs, Rose screamed. She wept when the Elder tossed aside its clothing and the few shreds of flesh that still covered it.

"Stop your blubbering," the Elder said, scampering along the edge of the mattress seeking the precise position to ensure a flawless impregnation. "Soon, you'll give life to my children." It wound a slick tentacle around each of her arms. Rose looked at it, trying to hide her repulsion, fearing it might take offense.

"I didn't know vampires could have children..."

"Oh, Rose," it said, though she could no longer see how it spoke. She wondered if it possessed telepathy, as its voice seemed to emanate from inside her skull. "Don't you get it yet? We aren't vampires. I'm surprised that a woman in this age would fall for such fairy tales."

Tentacles now danced over Rose's flesh, caressing and pressing, covering her with a sticky fluid. They pulled the denim jacket from her arms, unfastened the pink bra, and sent it sailing across the room. She felt a pinprick in her buttocks and then another in her thigh. Another pierced her right breast. She looked down to see that needle-thin appendages jutted from the end of each tentacle.

"What are you?" she finally asked, her head swimming as toxins filled her bloodstream.

"We're aliens, dear," the Elder said, his one eye glaring at his mate. "Instead of staging costly invasions, when we wish to conquer a world, one of us is sent to breed with the indigenous population, cultivating a hybrid race which eventually overwhelms the natives. I was the first of my race to arrive. I have sired four thousand offspring since my arrival."

"And Alex?"

"He was the runt of my most recent litter. He's been using the vampire routine for a century now." The Elder stood up and backed away from the side of the bed. Rose knew that it had finished, knew that it was too late to escape. The alien lumbered around the room, picking up bits of its discarded skin. Gradually, it pieced together its human façade. "Poor Alex – he always gets too attached to his mates. He can't bear to watch his own spawn devour their host."

The End

Hrothgar by Lee Clark Zumpe

Heorot trembled beneath a foul curse
The subject of which was once put to verse;
Hrothgar sought courage to vanquish his foe
But what caused the blight the text does not show.
Beowulf came, knew what he had to do,
(Heroes aren't known for thinking things through);
With no need for proof, he tracked down the thing,
Butchered poor Grendel, which obliged the king;
And, unfulfilled with the count of one dead,
The hero then lopped off Grendel's mom's head!
Mind you, it turns out that Hrothgar had lied:
It seems not one of his peasants had died.
King Hrothgar was once poor Grendel's best friend
Until one day that all came to an end.
Hrothgar is rarely driven by whim,
But never offend him during a swim.
Poor Grendel had made one crucial mistake:
Grendel was slaughtered for fouling the lake.

Girls on the Road
by
Sandy DeLuca

Mia Dragon…

It was her stage name. I didn't know her real one. Never asked.

My traveling companion … a partner in the odd, the perverse … the insane … in *that* time of my life.

I remember the dates, like I remember the guys — the ladies — and all the cities and towns where we went. I remember how I felt when I picked up my camera and shot their photos — ringside, backstage — at breakfasts and luncheons dedicated to people gone into the ether of time … their portraits left incomplete…

I recall a trip to Pennsylvania, vivid smells of cold and smoke, early winter. We drove through the Appalachians — and it looked like snow rose up out of the road. I thought it was strange, a magical phenomenon. And when I looked down mountainous trails, I saw towns with glowing lights, December dreamlands — starry realms of the imagination. I saw dark there too — dead deer at the side of the highway — a wolf's head, bloodied fur frozen to the ground, dead eyes glowing yellow — and I wondered where the rest of its body lay. At the bottom of the steep mountainside? Devoured by something larger and deadlier — something wandering through that snow rising from the pavement?

Those sights — the acrid smells — the way the sky seemed close — ominous — all of it awed me. And when I told the town people, they just shrugged like it wasn't a big deal. They'd seen it countless times — just like I'd seen high tides and seagulls swooping down for food on boat rides to Block Island.

Mia Dragon drove — she drove a lot — although she stopped to add water to her car's radiator, oil to her engine…countless times before we got anywhere. But she assured me, with her athletic body moving quickly, "Nothing can go wrong, kid. We'll get there — we'll get back."

And we did.

I captured faces, events, color and art on film reels. I recorded words, the truth … even lies.

Mia wore spandex, high boots, black hair long and wild. Crimson streaked her flesh and the crowd cried out.

Memphis … Manhattan … Boston. The noise, dialects, the smells, all diverse. Hotels, fast food, soaring down freeways … over bridges … in Mia's beat-up car.

And the days and nights ran together like surreal dreams … the lovers … the towns … but it ended, gradually, eerily, like dead rising from graves. Ambling towards us, like years that go by too quick, like all finales … bitter and sweet.

But, on certain nights … when the owl shrieks and December wind howls … we're still girls on the road, creaking bones and shaking limbs … raven wings flap above us … Mia gives up one last pose.

…Azrael is close behind.

The End

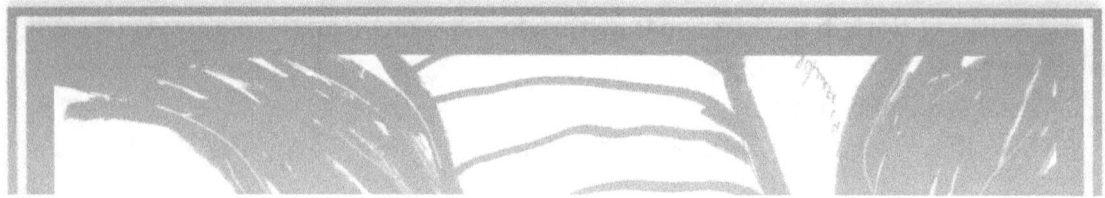

Mike Walker in Byberry
by
Linda Barrett

When the sun crept into the west for the evening, Mike Walker ran a brush through his curly blond hair before his apartment's hallway mirror. Adjusting his thick, wire-framed glasses, he studied his image. The plain, gold cross which hung from his neck shone in the setting sun's slanted light.

He prepared himself to cast out demons from the remains of Byberry State Hospital. Dusk arrived, heralding Mike's moment. People in his church told him only invoking Christ's name could cast out demons. Mike considered them foolish. He had the Holy Spirit in him. He could do it himself.

Mike left his apartment and skipped down the complex's stairs. He walked across the parking lot and waited for the traffic to allow him to pass. Byberry used to stand right there until two decades ago.

The infamous state hospital lay in rubble under a thick, black forest of trees and thickets. Mike took in the smell of wet, rotting grass and leaves as he lifted the darkness-defying yellow caution tape surrounding the trees. He hummed hymns that he learned from his childhood and even when the dual diagnosis of bipolar and schizophrenia overtook his life during his under-graduate college days.

The doctors his parents took him to see insisted he take medication. All the psychotropic drugs the doctors fed him only made him a sleepy easy target for the demons to attack him. He read about them coming back into him after he cast them out. They always came back to him to revisit him.

His pastor friend, Clinton Ah, explained to Mike until he was breathless that only Jesus could cast out the demons. Clinton said repeatedly Christians could not be possessed by the devil.

Mike always consulted his Bible to show him that when someone had his demons cast out, the demons would come back into that person again.

"Why do you insist that you can fight demons?" Clinton asked him. "Why do you always believe you don't need medication for your illness? These demons are part of your delusion."

As Mike stepped under the yellow tape, he scoffed at Clinton's advice. How could he fight the demons when he believed himself a new Messiah? The voices in his head always told him that. Mike spent all night without sleep, searching for the Bible verse that illustrated his belief about being repossessed.

"I don't need medication to fight the demons. I have the Holy Spirit within me to cast them out," he said.

He looked around him to see only rain-wet weeds and trees. A rusted wrought iron bench lay on its ornate, scrolled back. Mike stepped through the leaf-covered forest floor to look at it.

White teeth shone dimly underneath a patch of dark ivy. Mike reached out to touch them.

"Don't touch those!" a voice whispered at his left.

Mike stood up and looked at the dark form standing a few feet before him. The figure resembled a man with his arms at his sides. He was encrusted in dirt and leaves. Mike noticed the wide-eyed gaze in the man's eyes.

"Who are you?" Mike asked.

"She was killed here. I found her first. Those are her teeth," the man said.

"Where's the rest of her?" Mike gasped. His skinny legs shook with fear.

The leaf-encrusted man raised his grimy hoe blade.

"Bill strangled her. He cut her up and buried her body throughout the garden. We're going to grow her." He gestured with the hoe. "We're going to plant those teeth. Grow a whole crop of girls from Ward D."

Mike mustered up his strength and stood upright. He knew a demon when he encountered one.

"I cast you out!" he hollered at the man, aiming a finger at him.

The man raised his hoe and charged at Mike. Mike raised the cross around his neck and squinted from behind his glasses. The man disappeared into dust.

Brushing himself off, Mike walked on through the forest. In the pitch black darkness, Mike adjusted his eyes. He came across the remains of walls and doorways. His ears picked up screams from all around him. Phantoms of people in straightjackets or huddling in corners surrounded him. A black-haired woman rushed up to him with terrified, dark eyes.

"You've come, young man," she whispered.

Mike looked at her gauzy nightgown.

"I cast you out!" he shouted.

She twisted before him and opened her mouth in a scream. He walked through her and came face to face with a man in a doctor's coat wearing a reflector around his head. The stooped-over older man stared at Mike from behind his horn-rimmed glasses.

"Are you ready for your operation?" the doctor asked.

Mike raised his cross from around his neck.

"I cast you out!" he shouted.

He traveled through phantoms and dark rooms. A nurse in a white suit from the 1950s turned away from the remains of a medicine cabinet. She held out a tray to him.

"Time for your medicine," she said with a skull for a face.

Mike stretched out his arms.

"I cast you out!"

The nurse turned away from Mike and shouted, "Doctor! He's violent!"

Two orderlies came up and made a barrier around Mike. They grabbed him by his arms and hoisted him off the leaf-strewn remains of a cement floor. He couldn't shout out anything. What was going on here? He had the Holy Spirit in him, but the demons had conquered him again.

Mike found himself dragged through crumbled remains of hallways by these powerful demons.

Nothing but air came through his open mouth. Demonic forces surrounded him. He stared at them in gaping horror as their faces leered at him. The very air he breathed escaped him, smothered by their foul-smelling stenches.

14

The gnarled orderlies threw Mike into a narrow, little room with blood-red walls. Slamming the door after him and locking it with a click, they left him on the floor with its scrawled graffiti. Mike still could not close his mouth.

"Welcome," a small, young voice said.

Mike looked up to see a small, black-haired little boy looking out a window with a chain-link curtain. He still couldn't speak. The boy still looked out the window.

"Mike Walker," the boy said in his high-pitched voice, which sounded mocking. "You can't fight demons. We're too powerful for your faith. You don't have enough of it."

Mike looked around the room at the garish, blood-colored walls. His mouth muscles still hurt because he couldn't close them.

"You must remember you cannot leave here. You dared to come here out of your own foolishness."

Mike watched as the boy turned his head. He managed to emit a gasp.

The boy had black sockets where his eyes used to be.

"You're here forever in this outpost to Hell," he calmly told Mike.

Mike felt his mouth. He placed his hands on the sides of his face and tried pressing his jaws together. He pounded the top of his head with his fists to get his mouth to close. His fingers massaged his cheeks. His hands pulled out his tongue. Nothing seemed to work.

"Mike Walker," the boy said, standing with his arms stiff at his sides. "You cannot speak. You have no power anymore. You came here of your own free will. No one can cast us out."

Mike pressed his back against the wall and wailed. He punched his jaws, but nothing happened.

The boy crawled on the floor towards Mike. He approached him upon his belly. His features narrowed until they morphed into a serpent. Mike pressed himself against the wall but could not escape the serpent-boy. The serpent-boy entered Mike's open mouth in a slow, gliding motion. Mike gagged.

"In Jesus's name," Mike managed to say. "I cast you out!"

The serpent slid out and became a boy again. The scarlet-walled door thrust itself open with a powerful force. The boy pressed himself against the window. He opened his mouth and emitted a piercing scream. Walls blew away and a brilliant light expanded everywhere.

Mike sat alone in the middle of the light.

A bearded man in white robes stood over him.

He laughed at Mike.

"Mike Walker," he said wryly. "You should know you can't cast out demons in your own name. A devil can't possess you if you belong to me. You have to cast out demons in my name because only I have that power."

Mike lowered his head in a contrite manner.

"Thank you for telling me that. Forgive me for trying to do things on my own."

The bearded man planted a rough, calloused hand with a deep nail hole in its palm.

"Go and live out your life in my name, Mike." he said and turned into the light.

Mike got to his feet.

"I think I'll do just that," he said and walked back to his apartment.

The End

Paranoia Strikes Deep by Marc Shapiro

I just found out
That I have two followers
On Instagram
Don't know where I got them
Don't know where they've been
But all of a sudden
They're in my techno crosshairs
It's cool for a bit
Then it's not
Paranoia strikes deep
Who
Are they
Why
Follow me
What
Do they want
Are they
Fans
Or fanatics
Groupies
Are they deep
Are they hot
Or worse yet
Are they monsters
Will they knock on the door
In the middle of the night
Are they bloodsuckers
Who lust for my efforts
Do they want me
To join them
In an eternity of blood rites
Before cutting me up
And scattering the pieces
Over five states
Well that lets the wind
Out of my sails
Time to unfriend

Awkward Blind Date by Matthew Wilson

Lonely vampire hunter
Meeting blind date
Keeping warm in her cape.

Hokey Pokey
by
Ken Goldman

"Well, lookin' back on it, I'd guess the idea must've seemed a bit crazy even to a couple of young-sters. But it was just kids bein' kids, you know, and sometimes boys get caught up in the moment, when doin' what's crazy seems like the only thing to do ..."

Eliaja Woodman, age 73
Caretaker of Mt. Mariah Cemetery

Jordy sat with Tag upon the rusted porch swing behind the old farmhouse. A brisk wind tousled the older boy's hair, its chill an unwelcome forecast of the winter to come. "Did you forget what today is?" he asked his kid brother.

Tag focused on the thickening clouds riding the bleeding autumn sky. "Nope. I didn't forget it's Dad's birthday. There's not much point to remembering, though, is there?"

The younger boy had not spoken much about his father during the past few months, but his brother had caught him crying in his room on more than one occasion. Jordy had taken the death even worse. Dead parents have the nasty tendency to haunt their sons, and more than a year after severe cardiac failure had claimed Elliott Darnell, his father's dying seemed all the boy talked about.

"How old would Dad have been?" Tag asked.

"Don't know. Old."

Jordy would not let the topic drop until he had explored new territory yielding fresh explanations of a universe that had done this to him. Recently, he had difficulty remembering details of his dad's face, and even the sound of his voice was slipping away. He worried that maybe soon there would be nothing left.

"You ever think about what he looks like under the ground, Tag? If Dad looks the same, the way we remember him?"

The sun was descending behind the western hills, and Tag seemed reluctant to take his attention from the sky, as if some precious moment might be lost. He hesitated before his eyes found his brother's.

"That's a weird thing to be thinking about. There's a decent sunset this evening. Why not let's just watch it?"

The older boy allowed the sky's palate of colors to carry him to some other place, but the distraction did not last. No October twilight could rival the shadowy denizens lurking in-side.

["Your father is dead, Jordy, and his rotting corpse is alone and unloved stinking in his grave ..."]

"I've just been wondering, is all. Maybe bugs got into his coffin. Maybe he's still wearing those damned horned-rimmed glasses over empty holes where his eyes were."

"We buried him wearing those horned rims, didn't we? I don't think Dad took them off after we put him into the ground. It's his birthday, so I'd rather not think about insects crawling out of his sockets, okay?"

The older boy kept silent for a moment. So much about death made no sense. Where was the logic behind placing eyeglasses on his dead father's face the day of the funeral? Tag had mentioned this was just a way to make his corpse more closely resemble the living man his family had known, but wasn't this a lie that made death seem like something it wasn't?

[" ... *stinking in his grave ...*"]

Jordy hated these dark passages through which his thinking led him. He dug deep for one of the good memories.

"You remember that song he used to sing with us, Tag? The one he taught us how to do with our hands and feet?"

" ... and our asses? That stupid Hokey Pokey song? How could I forget?"

He sang a few words under his breath.

"You put your right foot in, you put your right foot out
You put your right foot in, and you ..."

The memory of a birthday party washed over Jordy. He and a dozen friends had entangled themselves in a riotous knot during his dad's quickening Hokey Pokey lyrics and motions. Everyone was laughing; some kids were even falling. It was a wonderful moment, one worth remembering. But he had almost forgotten.

"A piece of Dad's soul might still be buried with him, you know. Something must be left of him the bugs can't get to. Something not flesh and bone."

Tag's eyebrow raised in that skeptic's fashion that informed you that you were full of shit. "What's with Dad is dirt and worms, maggots, cockroaches, and slugs! Maybe some skin is left, like a chewed-up dog bone, but that's all. Shit, Jordy! You're going on fifteen. That's almost two years older than me. Use your damned head."

Tag's few glimpses at anything dead consisted of the roadkills they occasionally discovered on the highway. Once, he had complained that death was bloody and it smelled bad. The night their dad had collapsed at dinner, the guys who came with the ambulance just tossed a sheet over his body as if what lay under were too awful to look at.

"Well, I think his soul is still down there ... or somewhere. I think there's more to being dead than just worms and dog bones, Tag. I don't know exactly what's left, but there's someone who's looking after Dad, making sure he's okay." Saying this did not make Jordy fully believe it, but the words helped. "Maybe you feel like going up to Mt. Mariah with me to find out? I mean, just so we can know what's what?"

The words just came out; Jordy didn't know from where. Maybe he had been waiting to speak them all along. He expected his kid brother to respond with shock or disbelief over his suggestion with all its grisly implications, maybe calling him a regal asshole for even mentioning it. But Tag seemed curious.

"You mean dig him up?"

"Just to be sure."

"Take Dad out of the ground?"

"That's what I'm saying."

"Now, let me get this straight. You're telling me we should just hike up to that ol' bone-yard with shovels right now and disturb Dad's grave?"

"Uh-huh."

Tag took a moment as if testing the depths of his own conscience.

"You know how wrong that is? Mom would kill us."

"It's Friday. Ladies' Night at The Buck-Eye. Mom won't even know."

Jordy hoped the same pre-pubescent demon that had spoken for him might whisper to his brother.

["Well, why not? Why the hell not? You want to know, don't you? Just like when you sneak a peek at those roadkill cats smeared like bloody pancakes ..."]

"Maybe I'll just go up there with you to see you do it. 'Cause I know you're just talkin' the talk and you won't do it, Jordy. Not in a billion years."

"Well, we won't know about that 'till we get there, will we?"

"This is so wrong ..."

"Maybe. Maybe not."

The brothers shook on it, demonstrating their honorable intentions were not the least bit contaminated with the curiosity that a dead father's remains would look pretty ripe after so many months. That would be a terrible reason to hike up to the old Mt. Mariah graveyard using their father's own toolshed shovels to do the job.

You had to respect the dead. But you had to know the truth too.

Dad deserved that much.

****

The last trace of daylight had abandoned the sky as the brothers approached Mt. Mariah's rear entrance. Each tossed a shovel over the high iron gate that surrounded the old bone-yard. Climbing a nearby oak, they scaled the barrier. Roving shadows played mindfuck games as the boys searched the jagged rows of headstones for their father's burial site. Although the grass was freshly manicured, a cemetery becomes a different place at night. Its amenities went unnoticed in the uncertain moonlight as the boys wandered the lumpy grounds amid the tombstones.

Finally, the familiar inscription appeared.

Elliott P. Darnell
October 20, 1953 - August 19, 1999
Beloved Husband and Father

"You're okay with this?" Jordy asked. "'Cause once we start, there's no changing your mind."

"I'm okay," Tag said, but he didn't sound like he was.

The older brother broke ground first. Tag needed a moment to digest the significance of their act, then set himself to the task. Together the two attacked the earth made soft by a recent gully washer. One brother eyed the other, each seeking silent encouragement, a voiceless agreement that what they were doing would not ram them both directly into hell.

After an hour's work, Jordy broke the silence first.

"You put your left hand in, you put your left hand out
You put your left hand in, and you shake it all about ..."

Keeping his voice low, Tag joined him, and they sang as they shoveled, prodding out clods of damp earth in time to the rhythm.

" ... You do the hokey pokey, then you turn yourself around
That's what it's all about!"

Laughing, the brothers headed into another chorus with more enthusiasm.

"You put your right hand in, you put your right hand out
You put your right hand in, and you--"

Jordy's shovel struck something solid. Each looked to the other in the night's stillness. Something vibrated beneath their feet. It wasn't much, but for one terrible moment, the brothers froze where they stood.

" ... and you ... shake it ... all about ..."

Standing inside the deep hole, Jordy looked to Tad for confirmation of what he had heard.

[You?]

His brother shrugged.

[Not me ...]

In the darkness, they could feel the edge of the coffin's lid through the dirt below. Tag attempted a forced smile that aborted itself at once. He tried whispering but could only gasp his next words.

"Let's put both our feet the hell out of this hole, okay? And I'm not talking about the hokey pokey, Jordy."

His brother's remark made the older boy break into convulsed laughter. Tag was no match for the moment's heebee-jeebies and, along with his brother, shook so hard with his own nervous cackling he had to hold his stomach to keep from losing his dinner.

The soft dirt beneath quivered. Something seemed to shift its weight as if the soil had heaved and swelled. The thick mud made solid footing tricky, and it was difficult to tell.

"He's right below us. We can do this, Tag, but we have to do it together. Are you with me?"

"Let's just leave while we still--"

But the older boy already had decided. He crouched to his knees, moving closer to the sunken casket, then looked back to Tag.

"It's only Dad under here, you know."

He returned to the song in the manner it was meant to be sung, slowly, the way he had heard his father at weddings and birthday parties.

"You-put-your-left-leg-in, you-put-your-left-leg-out
You-put-your-left-leg-in, and-you-shake-it-all-about ..."

Jordy nodded for his brother to help him out. The younger boy's lips moved, but no words came. He had better luck with his second attempt. Together they managed a shaky rendition of the next line.

"You do ... the hokey pokey ... and you shake it all around ..."

Jordy shoveled great clumps of sticky earth from the casket. Taking his brother's cue, Tag did the same. When the entire top portion of the pinewood box appeared, Jordy maneuvered his ear close to the lid as if eavesdropping on a conversation.

"I think something's moving inside. Listen."

Tag followed his brother's instruction, kneeling in the soft mud closer to the coffin.

"I don't hear anything. Maybe it's just bugs. Or rats."

"Listen better, twerp! I'm telling you there's something moving in there!"

Tag's ear brushed the cheap knotted pine of the coffin's lid. The wood was not especially thick, and he pressed his cheek against it to hear if there were anything.

"Jordy, I swear if you're fucking with me ..."

Tag suddenly pulled his face away from the pinewood and jumped, falling backward. He skittered as far as he could propel himself in reverse while on his ass.

"I heard a thump. Christ, Jordy, I think he's trying to push the top open! I just felt him hit the goddamn lid!"

"Can you see anything? I can't tell. It's too-"

The coffin's hinges creaked. Its top might have slipped a bit over the lip, then fell back again with a thud, but in darkness, nothing seemed certain. The rusted metal of the hinges moaned one more time, and this time the lid gave way. A sudden breeze kicked up, carrying with it the stench of rotted meat.

[...alone and stinking in his grave, Jordy ... stinking in his grave ...]

"D-Dad?" Jordy managed.

"Right foot ... in ... right foot ... out ..."

"I think he's sitting up, Jordy - - I think he's ..."

"I can't tell -- it's too dark to see any--"

Something landed in Jordy's lap, and he held it close to his face to examine. The night did not permit a clear view, but touching the object left no doubt. He handed it to his brother.

"His glasses?" Tag asked.

"I think so. Yes, I think--"

" ... you do ... the ... hokey pokey ..."

Tag dropped the horned-rims into the mud.

"I want to go, Jordy. I want to get the hell out of here now!"

"Not yet ..." The older boy leaned close to the coffin and whispered, "It's us, Dad. Tag and Jordy."

"Christ, Jordy!"

"We just wanted to say happy birthday, Dad."

"Oh shit, Jordy! Let's just-"

"I'm way ahead of you, Tagger."

Jordy climbed out of the hole first, pulling his brother free. From below, he heard another gurgling attempt at speech.

"That's ... what it's ... all about ... all ... about ..."

The older boy took a last look into the opened grave trying to determine something, anything. The darkness would not permit it.

Finally, he said, "We're going now, Dad." He looked to his brother.

Tag hesitated, then stepped closer to the hole.

"See ya."

They ran all the way home.

****

The expected phone call came early in the morning. Some old guy asking to speak to Florence Darnell identified himself as Eliaja Woodman, the caretaker at Mt. Mariah, and he mentioned how the grave belonging to her late husband had been vandalized during the night.

Finding answers did not require astute detective work. The brothers had dragged sludge into the kitchen while layers of dried muck saturated their clothing. The two insisted they had been mud wrestling near the pond, but the old guy on the phone had another shoe to drop. He had found shovels inside their father's opened grave, and the initials E.P.D. carved into the handles provided smoking gun evidence. The boys admitted what they had done, but there seemed no sane reason to tell what they had seen. They had pissed off enough people already.

Their mother was among them, but her anger didn't last long. The tears did, and old Eliaja had to soften his own anger considerably to prevent the young widow from becoming outright hysterical.

"They're just kids bein' kids, is all," Woodman remarked, and he asked the woman to go easy on her two boys. The old guy assured her no permanent damage had been done and that he had no desire to pursue the matter further. He asked if he might have a moment to speak to the older boy.

Florence Darnell held out the receiver for her son. Lip synching a feeble "I'm sorry, Mom," the boy approached the phone as if she were handing him a dead rat.

"Is this Jordy I'm speakin' to?" Eliaja asked.

"Yes, sir ..."

"It's only us two on the line, is that so, son?"

"Yes, sir."

"That's good, son, that's real good. Now just in case your mama is in the room, I want you to keep 'Yes Sirring' me and listenin' real good. You hear me talkin' to you, Jordy?"

"Uh huh ... sir."

"That was a real terrible thing you and your brother done last night. But you already know that much, so that's not what this is about. I want you listenin' to me now like you ain't never listened to nobody before. I mean with both ears turned to high volume."

"Yes ..."

"All right, then, here it is. You ain't gonna do no more grave visitin' on my shift, son. You and your kid brother is gonna keep off Mt. Mariah's grounds 'cept durin' reg'lar visitin' hours, or I'll show you some real hokey pokey. And that's what it's all about ..."

The old man cackled like a mad elf. His voice suddenly seemed oddly familiar.

"Now put your mama back on the phone, boy, so we can wrap this damned mess up proper."

Within minutes, Jordy had fastened the lock inside his room for the first time since his father's funeral. He knew a lecture was coming, but for now, he had something inside his head that demanded serious reflection. His brain replayed the same scene like a rewound video.

... Eliaja Woodman discovers two boys digging up a grave and he hears them muttering some shit about the hokey pokey. The damage has already been done to Elliott P. Darnell's plot, so the old fart is just goosing up a little payback for himself by scaring the bejeezus out of the vandals who have had the balls to ravage the grounds he's responsible for. The geezer hides himself behind a nearby headstone and throws his voice in the dark like one of those old-time ventriloquists working with a dummy, knowing how the dark plays mean tricks on a couple of spooked kids whose imaginations are already into hyper-drive. Old Eliaja laughs himself sick watching the two vandals practically fudge their pants.

It was a stretch, of course, but who could say it didn't happen that way? Jordy hadn't seen anything he could swear to, and Tag was just a kid who watched too many vampire movies. This revised version made a whole lot more sense than a dead man climbing out of his coffin to do the hokey pokey. No, Dad wasn't trapped inside that pinewood box. His soul was floating around somewhere in heaven, looking down on him and Tag, safe with Jesus and his angels while God watched over him. Hell, this was what everyone else believed, wasn't it? What lay beneath the dirt at Mt. Mariah wasn't really his dad. Not anymore.

So why even bother giving a second thought about where those dumb-ass horned-rimmed glasses came from?

Or that awful smell ...

****

Eliaja Woodman held a pair of eyeglasses as he spoke to the woman on the phone. He did not especially like nodding and smiling like an idiot, but the words he uttered called for it.

"Yes, I think we can put the matter behind us, Mrs. Darnell. I wouldn't go too hard on your boys. In time, I'm sure both Jordy and Tag will come to understand what they did was just an expression of the grief any youngster feels for a lost parent. You take care now."

Woodman returned the phone to its cradle, and removing a ragged kerchief from his hip pocket, he mopped sweat from his brow. It had been a long night, and there was work to be done at the Darnell plot. The diggers would be arriving any time now to put things back the way they were, so he would have to be quick.

"Fuckin' kids ..."

He studied the horned rims in his hands. Those damned eyeglasses came close to causing him some nasty trouble. He would have to be more careful about falling asleep so early during his shift.

"I guess you'll be wantin' these specs returned before the diggers get here. Must've fallen off your face durin' all that excitement, eh? I've got to put you back where you belong. I'm sorry, Elliott, I know it seems unfair, but Death, he don't make no concessions 'bout who he takes. Happy birthday."

He handed the horned rims to the rotting corpse that sat inside his small office.

Elliott P. Darnell indeed wanted his glasses.

He put his right hand out ...

The End

Waiting
by
Marge Simon

The bench is cold, the station deserted. She has no idea when the next train will arrive, or even if there are any trains left, still running. She knows she must get away from here, but she doesn't remember why.

The floor is littered with refuse –used condoms, cigarette butts. All around her is a dark fantasy out of Dahlgren, a depraved city of fallen angels, where the roads that lead here have no exit. She begins to count the tiles on the floor. She feels inexplicably dirty, defiled.

Distant and low, then louder –the wail of a train horn. The floor quakes with the rumble of wheels on steel. She jumps up, rushes to the rattling doors in time to see it thundering by. Then silence. There's something familiar about all of this. Her neck itches.

She returns to the cold bench. She has no idea when the next train will come, or why she should be on it. With a sigh, she resumes counting the tiles on the floor. The bench is cold. The itch returns. She begins to scratch her neck. Over and over, until the skin gives way and blood oozes to the surface. She knows the blood will attract vampires, but she no longer cares.

Another train and yet another rumble past, but none are stopping here. By now, a vampire is sitting next to her and she's too weak to scream. She remembers now, the trains to this station are always late, if they come at all.

The End

Shadows by Todd Hanks

Sometimes shadows leave our bodies,
stalking black like prowling panthers,
as surefooted as leopards leaping,
sliding as silently as hooded cobras.

The shadows live the fantasies
we keep buried deep beneath
the waves of our subconscious sea.

Then as if made from lulling twilight
the shadows slip back into the night,
transported away to bodies again,
to represent the dark within.

Veil of the Weary One
by
Lee Clark Zumpe

Bitter, unseasonable winds slithered through the barren avenues of Shatley Creek. Certain menacing shadows pitched their uncanny weight against the dull street lamps, and the moon crawled along impotently behind a thin layer of purple clouds. Dogs howled anxiously from the scattered farmsteads dotting the tiny Appalachian cove. The whine of big rigs traveling south along State Road 201 further up the slope of Richmond Mountain showered down over the valley.

Most of them never even noticed the turn-off for Shatley Creek, which was for the best. The townsfolk rarely welcomed strangers.

Colby arrived not long after midnight but long after the only diner in town had locked its doors and fed the rats in the alley. Darkened windows and empty sidewalks rolled by on either side. Shatley Creek was devoid of roving teenage gangs that might haunt a larger city on a Friday night; no drive-in theaters, bowling alleys, or late-night fast food stands offered them refuge here. The night was painfully lonely, as was he.

Colby drove cautiously down the main boulevard, still leery of small town police and unexpected speed traps. The chill in the air made it feel like late October. The summer he had left behind in Florida seemed a lifetime away. Here, everything seemed a lifetime away.

Everything except the Darklings.

Loathingly, Colby turned down Piney Lane and traced the steady stream of his high beams as they illuminated an elaborate wrought iron gate. The sign above the gate confirmed that he had made no mistakes. Spread before him was the final resting place known for more than two centuries as Serenity Gardens.

Colby parked before the gate and quietly got out of his rental car. The dusk embraced him the moment he abandoned the safety of the Dodge Sebring. He reached back in, retrieved a heavy knapsack from the passenger seat, and then closed the door gently. He stepped through a clot of weeds to reach the gate, his eyes mindfully drifting toward the ground.

He stopped.

They could be hiding anywhere, she had told him.

Those words had resonated through a dozen graveyards, melting like crystals of ice in the sun only to rise again from the stygian springs of twilight. He shuddered at an image of his former partner and lover, mauled and naked and shivering upon the cold earth – her eyes nothing more than black caverns ringed by crusted blood. Her dying words would plague him for the rest of his life, as much as her quest had become his own since they took her from him.

Colby hesitated for only a moment, burying both the warning and the image in his mind. As his fingers wound around the icy gate, a rustling of leaves and the eerie screech of an owl drew his gaze deep into the cemetery. The shadows beyond shuffled menacingly, coiling about ancient and crumbling headstones. Unchecked vegetation grew thick and high and obscured many of the markers. Litter congregated on the ground before the gate, seemingly eager to leave. Years of neglect were painfully apparent.

He suspected there was no one left who had reason to visit these graves. Either that or something here kept them from setting foot on the land. He wondered if the Darklings had infected the townsfolk with their grim apocalyptic nightmares.

The rusted chain that bound the gate remained intact. He might have managed to break the old thing with the tire iron in his trunk, but he did not want to make enough noise to stir the townsfolk. It would be best if they stayed tucked safely beneath their blankets, snug in their homes and far removed from the danger. Colby was lean and fit, and he quickly pulled himself up and over the wall.

Carefully, he struck out into the heart of the old graveyard. Eastern hemlocks stood solemnly between jagged rows of deteriorating headstones. Ghostly Indian pipe pushed through the blanket of fallen leaves, feeding on rotting herbage. Colby used his flashlight to read the fading names of the people laid to rest here. More interesting to him, though, were the dates. Many of these graves were hollowed out and refilled before the signing of the Declaration of Independence. Though history had failed to record it, Shatley Creek had been the first permanent settlement in the region. Its roots sank deep into the Appalachian ground.

Farther in from the gate, the underbrush grew wild and presumptuous. Witch hazel and striped maple clogged the narrow aisles between the grave markers. Christmas fern and poison ivy brushed against Colby's jeans. Again, he peered keenly into the tangle of brushwood, scanning the unrelenting darkness fearfully. Somewhere in this pitch lay a Darkling, its nebulous black bulk squatting in the shadows as its slithering tentacles spread through the night. In any blackened thicket, a Darkling might lurk – waiting, patiently, for a seeker to arrive.

A seeker like poor Andrea.

Seven years ago, they had met in Gatlinburg. He had been on vacation with his wife; Andrea was traveling east toward Emmett's Cove. During their brief encounter, she had fascinated him with her knowledge of Appalachian folklore. His interests lying in the same field, he set up a date for a lengthy interview with her to gather information for a book he was piecing together. Through sporadic correspondence, they grew close.

His marriage dissolved less than a year after that meeting, and in Andrea he had found new life – and more.

Andrea worked for a cryptic association that commissioned specialists to seek out specific artifacts. Her curious charge was to collect twenty-four interconnecting stones scattered throughout the Appalachians by pioneer homesteaders. These stones had originated in the Middle East before the birth of Christ and over the centuries had been passed down along a series of bloodlines. The custodianship of the pieces was of extreme importance. Arguments concerning their care had spawned a dozen wars. Sometime during the 15th Century, the stones passed into the hands of an occult scholar bound for the New World.

Initially, Colby had not understood the significance of the stones, and he had sought to convince Andrea to forsake her quest. After seeing one of the Darklings sent by the Great Old Ones to keep the stones from being reassembled, his opinion quickly changed. His faith in the secret history taught by Andrea's affiliates grew.

Now, his quest was almost at an end. Tonight, he would recover the twenty-fourth stone, and he could reassemble the ancient icon referred to as the Veil of the Weary One.

At length, Colby spotted the lone crypt standing near the center of the cemetery. Small and modest, the black-stoned sepulcher had no equal within a hundred miles. It seemed grotesque and alien in its surroundings, a dark malignancy even more grim than its somber surroundings.

The ancient door clung precariously from rotten hinges.

Colby risked the dank gloom that had resided in that crypt for centuries. His flashlight lurched ineffectively into the depths. Slowly he eased down the steps. The black walls closed in on either side as he descended.

They could be hiding anywhere.

The Darklings had been spawned by dark forces in the distant past. Long ago, their influence upon earth had been far greater. They subjugated humanity from their secreted lairs, directing their followers through commands conveyed in dreams. They controlled the course of history for many ages.

Their reign ended only when a cosmic traveler chanced upon the earth and discovered the sinister enslavement of humankind. This benefactor who slew most of the Darklings came to be known as the Weary One – for his relentless war with the Darklings to liberate humanity lasted five thousand years. At the end of his crusade, when the few remaining Darklings surrendered, he had grown so tired he sat down upon the earth and closed his eyes. He told the newly freed humans he wished to sleep for five thousand years, and, having said so, he turned to stone.

The last Darklings found the Weary One sometime later, and, out of anger, shattered the stone into twenty-four pieces.

These pieces have been coveted by humans and Darklings alike ever since. Humans strive to keep track of the pieces, so the Weary One can be roused from his long repose to complete the task of cleansing the world of the Darklings. The Darklings seek to keep the pieces from being reunited, for they fear retribution.

The Darklings, now, had more to lose than ever before. Their numbers had swelled again during the Weary One's absence, and a New Dark Aeon ushered in by the imminent arrival of their forebears guaranteed the Darklings would have power once more.

Colby detested the Darklings for what they had done to humanity – for what they had done to Andrea.

Something curled around his ankle.

He jumped, falling to one side. His shoulder struck the wall, and he began to pitch forward. The thing tightened its grip on his leg as he fought to keep his balance.

As he plunged forward, sliding along the slimy moss-covered wall, he aimed his flashlight toward his leg. Slender ebon tentacles wormed their way out of the darkness and clustered around his feet. Another one crept up his leg.

Somehow, he managed to stay upright and finally reached the floor of the crypt. Desperately he scanned the room, knowing that in some corner, the main body of the Darkling lay hidden. He began hacking at the flailing tentacles with a Bowie knife. Bits of meat and spatters of acidic black blood sprayed into the musty air.

As he fought to destroy the Darkling, his thoughts drifted back to his love. Andrea had met her fate in a similar sepulcher. He never forgave himself for losing her. He still heard her screams every night beneath the stars – still heard her cries echoing across the great gulfs of dark matter, resonating from distant knots of interstellar dust where the hideous hosts of the Darklings hold stolen souls in vast reservoirs for their Masters.

They had enslaved her. He could only begin to imagine the agonies she had suffered.

The Darkling had retracted more of its tentacles from the graveyard to keep Colby from recovering the stone. Its efforts renewed, Colby grew frantic. His knife chopped wildly at the writhing appendages, scoring notches of mangled black flesh. His attacks became increasingly more reckless. He felt his own blade sink into his leg, and he howled.

Just then, the Darkling's eyes flashed, sensing his pain. Colby, though badly hurt, saw the dark crimson orbs pulsing in the corner. He spun around and leaped toward it. From his pack, he pulled a can of lighter fluid and a book of matches. In an instant, he had doused the Darkling. It shrieked and thrashed from side to side, lashing him with its tentacles.

He lit a match and flicked it toward the ghastly horror.

The flames consumed the loathsome creature, and it shuddered as it died a fiery death. As the thing burned, the blaze rendered a dull orange glow which sent the shadows in the chamber scurrying. Colby approached the altar, where the last piece of the puzzle rested.

From his knapsack, he removed all the pieces he had recovered previously. Working attentively, Colby began to piece together the relic. Though the group which had commissioned the crusade would undoubtedly be angered that he had done so, Colby intended to be the one who roused the Weary One – he had to know that Andrea had not been sacrificed for the sake of an empty myth.

The twenty-four pieces lay spread across the cold altar. Colby stared at them curiously. He had been offered no guide to assembling the stone. There were no instructions, no written words to assist him. He only knew that putting the pieces together correctly would reanimate the Weary One. The legend did not even suggest what form the Weary One would take, though it was rumored that its appearance was cast from the images it found in the minds of those who sought its aid.

As he slaved over the reconstruction, he heard them. Outside, shambling through the dusk, more Darklings approached. The things had heard the dying wails of their brother as they patrolled the dismal graveyard, and now they sailed toward the crypt to avenge him. Colby eyed the steps anxiously, his fingers struggling to match the pieces scattered across the altar.

As the first dozen tentacles crept into the room, and as the black form of Darkling shadowed the pale moonlight floating lethargically through the doorway, Colby recognized the pattern of the pieces before him. Frantically, he assembled them, even as a slick feeler coiled about his ankle.

Colby fit the final stone into place.

The crypt was flooded with blinding light, and Colby tottered back away from the altar. His hands covered his eyes as the brilliant radiance pulsed. The Darkling disintegrated as the light bathed it, screaming morbidly into the night. Its allies, still traversing the cemetery, must have drowned in the shimmering tide surging from the old sepulcher. Colby heard their pitiful wails.

Colby smiled and thought of Andrea as the Weary One began to form.

The End

Cayuga by Lee Clark Zumpe

Winter laid early siege to the lake,
with skies gravestone gray;
now the Wolf moon rolls across its crystallized face
sweeping the tears of its victims away.

The Forest
by
Anna Rose

Jesse was scared. So scared. Paul, the new neighbor boy who had moved into the old Sizney place in the past week, had taken him along on a hike into the forest. At first, Jesse had been proud that the older boy had invited him on the exciting adventure. It made him feel like he was so much more grown up than he was.

After letting him ride on the rack on the back of his bike, Paul had taken Jesse deep into the dense growth, where moss grew on the sides of the trees that received only minimal sunlight on their bark. It had seemed almost magical to the little boy, and he had touched and commented upon so much of what he observed.

Everything had gone well until Jesse fell and skinned one knee and the heel of one hand. Paul had run away, laughing as Jesse tried to keep up. After a futile attempt to catch up, Jesse had finally sat down on a fallen tree and started to cry. At the tender age of five, he was unfamiliar with how cruel some children can be.

It was starting to get dark now, and that only made the forest seem so much scarier than it was in the daylight hours. He could hear things moving about around him, things he couldn't see, and that frightened him even more than the monster under the bed did. At least with the monster under the bed, he could hide under his blanket, and it would not be able to reach him.

Here, he had no blanket. The monsters were out there, and he would be unable to protect himself from them.

When an owl hooted, Jesse just about jumped out of his skin. A moment later, he heard soft rustling in the leafy branches of a nearby tree.

"Paul?" he asked, hopeful that the boy had decided to come back. His nose was stuffy from all the crying he had been doing, making his voice sound funny, even to his own ears. "Is that you, Paul?"

There was no answer, just the sounds of the things that woke when the sun went down going about their business. Jesse shivered, clutching his arms around his chest as though he was giving himself a big hug.

It was starting to get chilly, and the cold fingers of fear sliding against his bare arms only made him shiver even more than he had been. When he'd left the house, it had been nice and warm out, and he had not needed even a light jacket.

That was not the case any longer.

Jesse rose, trying to orient himself in the direction from which he and Paul had entered the forest, but it all looked the same to him. His parents had never let him wander off on his own to play, and he would never have considered doing so, but he'd been very excited when the older boy had expressed a willingness to have him come along.

"Is anyone there?" he asked as he heard more things moving around in the forest. "I want to go home!"

The owl swooped down on noiseless wings, grabbing something from off of the forest floor. It glided a short distance and perched on a high branch, something dark and furry, with a long skinny tail, clutched in one clawed foot

"Hello, Mr. Owl," he said to the feathered sentry, forcing a tentative smile onto his lips. "Do you know the way out of here?"

At first, the creature seemed to consider his words. Jesse wondered if all owls looked so smart.

The owl's head twisted around as though it was part of a ball and socket setup. Daddy had shown him one of those when he went to visit him the last time at his garage. The owl reoriented its attention upon the curious boy, then turned to stare to its left.

"That way?" Jesse asked, turning and pointing in the direction the owl now faced.

There was no reply. When Jesse turned to face the owl again, it was gone, having flown away on its preternaturally silent wings.

"Mr. Owl?"

Silence except for a bit of fading birdsong in the distance.

Jesse marched off in the direction the owl had suggested. He knew the owl could not talk and probably did not understand what he had said, but, he reasoned as only a five-year-old child could, it did not hurt to take that chance.

Before long until the forest was so dark, he could not see his hand even when he held it up to his face. Even his bedroom did not get this dark when the lights were out, and his bedroom door was closed tight.

Jesse decided that it was best to hunker down where he was in the shelter of some fallen branches that seemed to be covered in a layer of dead, decomposing leaves that gave off some warmth of their own as they slowly broke down into their component parts

Feeling a bit hungry, he dug deep into his front pocket with a grubby hand and pulled a wrapped candy out. Not able to see what it was exactly, he unwrapped it, careful not to drop it, then sniffed the sweet's surface. Then he gave it a long, slow lick.

Butterscotch, he thought. Not great, but it was food, wasn't it? He popped it into his mouth and allowed it to sit on his tongue, swallowing his spit as the candy slowly melted there. Maybe he could fool his belly into thinking it was having more than it was. It was worth a try, wasn't it?

Remembering that littering was bad, he jammed the candy wrapper back down into his pocket, where it joined an interesting-looking smooth pebble and an eight-sided die he had found in the gutter next to the sidewalk.

Jesse lay awake a long time, listening for the sound of grown-ups coming to find him, but he only heard the sounds of the forest in the nighttime. It was scary, so he made himself as small as he could in an attempt to make himself less attractive to whatever monsters might lurk there.

In time, he fell asleep, too exhausted to keep his eyes open. He faded away while still hoping that an adult would find him and take him home.

When Jesse woke, it was still dark, but he was being carried, held close to someone's chest, his head resting on what felt like a bony shoulder.

Whoever held him had a firm but gentle grip on his small body. He had no fear of being dropped by accident. His rescuer's shoulder was clothed in a musty-smelling jacket that seemed like something from his grandpa's closet and a thought came to him.

"Daddy?" he asked. Whoever it was just kept on walking without replying. He could feel it as they moved around trees and the natural debris that covered the forest floor.

He took a deep smell at his rescuer's shoulder and smelt dirt and mildew.

"Are you taking me home?" he tried again.

Again, no answer, just steady, rhythmic footfalls.

Jesse felt scared and whimpered a little. The hand that supported his back shifted and then stroked him gently, patting his shoulder, giving him a bit of comfort and reassurance.

In time, his rescuer's even, sure steps lulled him back to sleep once more.

****

It was the low cry of horror that woke him. It sounded like Mommy.

When he opened his eyes, he saw his mother, eyes red and swollen from hours of crying, standing on the front porch.

"Mommy!" he cried, holding out his arms to her. "I got lost!"

His mother's mouth worked, no sound emerging, but she lurched forward and snatched her son from the arms of his rescuer. Holding him tight, she stepped backward.

Jesse turned to see his rescuer, the person who had carried him through the depths of the forest and then all the way home.

"Thank—," and he stopped short.

A fleshless, kepi-capped skull grinned at him. The cap's once vibrant blue coloring dulled to a nearly black color. A fat black beetle ran from one eyeless socket and across the bleached ridge of the skull's nose, then into the other socket to hide from the porch light.

"—you. I got scareded when Paul left me in the forest," he finished, always polite. Then he thought of something in the seemingly random way young children do. "Wait! I got something for you."

While his mother stared with fear and disbelief at her son's unlikely savior, Jesse reached into his pocket and pulled out his treasured eight-sided die. He then offered it to the creature, trust shining in his dark eyes. The skeleton reached out its gloved hand to the boy, palm-up, and the impromptu gift was dropped into it.

When the monster slipped the die into the breast pocket of its timeworn and rotting jacket, the boy's smile of pleasure could have brightened an abandoned mine shaft.

The rag-clad skeleton seemed to look at the boy, then cocked its head toward Jesse's mother. There was a question in those empty sockets, though she could not have said how she knew it was there.

She pointed.

"That house," she said, pointing at the old Sizney house, her voice uncharacteristically cold. "Paul lives there."

The skeleton seemed to give a nod, and then it lurched itself around to face the older boy's home.

"Uh—thank you," Jesse's mother said to the threadbare back, meaning it. The skeleton turned back to face her. She noted what looked like military insignia on its blue lapel and wondered how long ago the owner of these bones had died. "Thank you for me and for my son."

The skeleton sketched a salute at her, then turned back toward the Sizney house. She decided it was time to get indoors and give her son a much-needed scrub-up and then get him into bed before she called the police to let them know he had returned home safely.

****

Ten minutes later, she heard a long, horrified scream come from the direction of the Sizney home, but kept her attention on scrubbing the dirt out of her son's hair. At this point, it was really none of her business.

"Thank you for your service," she murmured in a tone too soft for Jesse to hear.

Her boy was home, safe, and that was all that mattered, wasn't it?

The End

Red Entry by Marc Shapiro

I have a big notebook
I use it to jot down
Ideas
Thoughts
Things to do
Things I forgot to do
Spur of the moments
That become this
This morning I went to a page
There were some notes scribbled from the previous day
No surprise there
There was a smear of dried blood
Bookmarking the next blank line
Yes, surprise there
I had no idea how it got there
Where was I
When this red came
I checked my body
For cuts
Bruises
Abrasions
Nothing
Then it dawned on me
I opened my mouth
Rubbed a finger across my teeth
It came back dripping red
Now I remember

The White Rose by Matthew Wilson

Never accept a white rose from a witch
Purple is the only color you should strive
If you are to pass the field of monsters
And so to greet the dawn alive

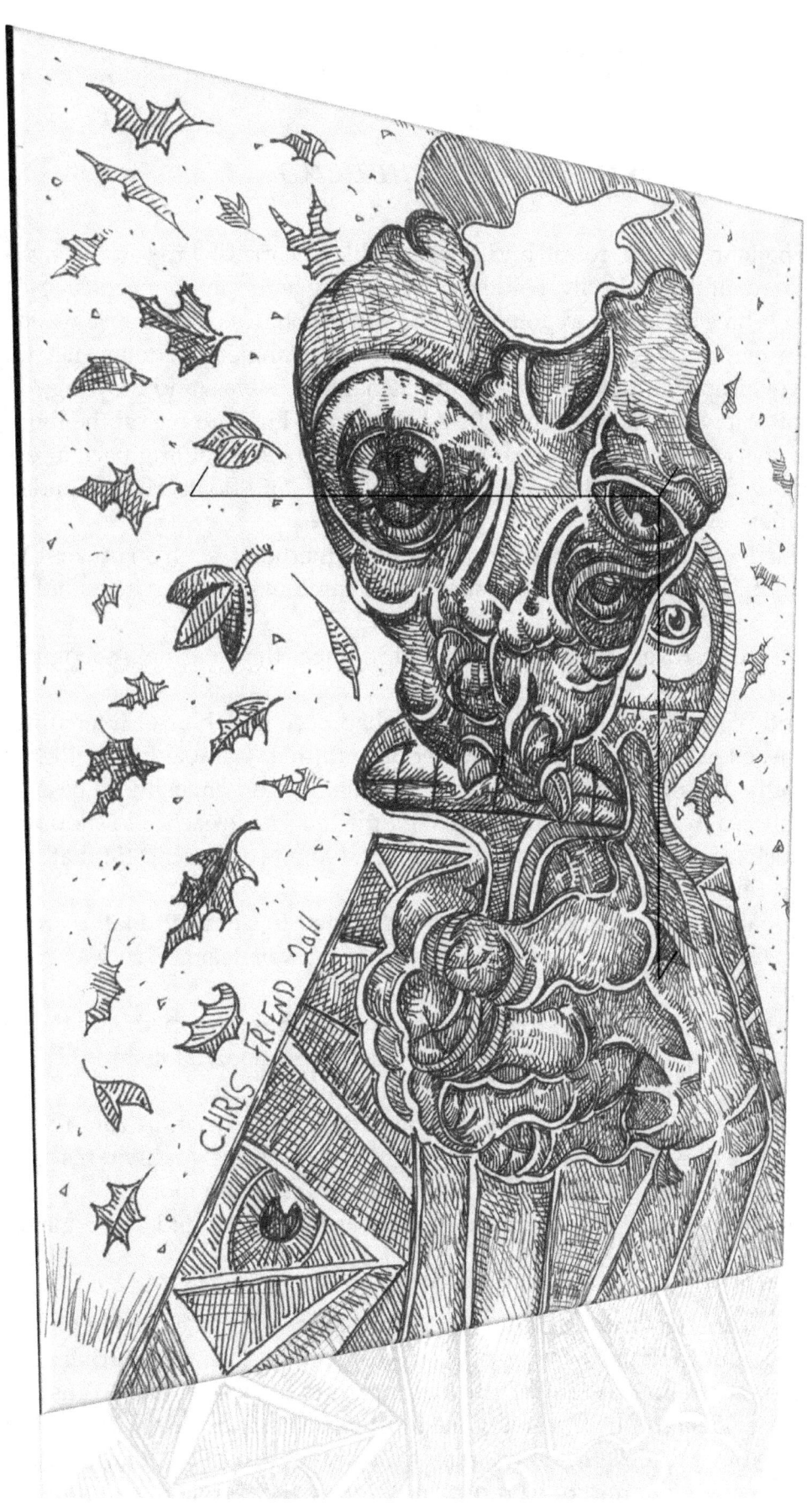

Hell-ium Balloon
by
Katherine Quevedo

The mylar balloon rotated, round and puckered like the mass of my stomach since giving birth. Light glared off the plain silver side while cartoony letters announced *Happy Mothers Day!!!* on the other. Three exclamation points and no apostrophe, of course. Aria wailed in my arms as I bounced her; my wrists contorted into unfamiliar angles to contain her tiny, hot, swaddled body. My biceps burned from the weight, small as she was (and growing).

"I didn't think it would lose air so fast," Abel muttered next to me on the living room couch. He tugged the white string, and the balloon dipped before settling back at eye level. "The guy at the store claimed he'd just filled it up. At least it still floats, right, Candace?" He grinned at me. "I mean, Mommy?"

The last thing I wanted was another reminder of motherhood, even on my first Mother's Day. My new title of Mommy and all its related forms came with the territory, but that balloon…

"It's a very nice gesture," I said, hoping he didn't hear the weariness seeping into my voice.

My days and nights the past couple of weeks had become a blur of interrupted sleep and meeting the needs of a new life incapable yet of gratitude—unable to support her own head! My body seethed at me for refusing to use formula, instead choosing to be Aria's sole food source. I'd tethered myself into a dire radius of time that made each solo shopping trip a race against the clock lest the little one wake up hungry. No one else could fill that role. How long until we could finally introduce solid food?

The crinkly balloon mocked me. One thought rotated in my head like it, around and around, glaring: *What have I gotten myself into?* I blinked away tears. This was not how a Mommy should feel.

The balloon slipped from Abel's grasp. He lunged for it and hopped onto the couch as the balloon rose, but new parenthood had made him sluggish, too, not just me. The balloon evaded him and settled at the peak of the vaulted ceiling with a soft *ploomf.*

An exasperated sigh escaped his lips. "I don't think I can reach it from the landing. Sorry, honey. It'll come down eventually, right?" So many questions qualified his statements these days, as if I could recognize better than him what was right anymore.

At least I wouldn't have to look at the balloon—as long as I could avoid glancing up, for each time I did, it seemed to stare back.

****

In her third week, Aria started sleeping through longer stretches of the night. Meanwhile, my mind struggled to shut down when it was supposed to sleep, and during the waking times, it felt as bleary as a rain-soaked windshield. It preoccupied me with concerns like how I looked to Abel with evidence of pain marring the most intimate parts of my body. Would we be able to touch each other again? Would we want to? My eyes avoided the mirror as much as possible. No point facing how grotesque I'd become. Not for the purple rings under my eyes, not even so much for that saggy expanse of belly resembling a relief map, the warped volcano of my navel—those were to be expected. I dreaded facing myself because it would force the realization that I was unfit in other ways.

One afternoon, as Abel bobbed Aria in his arms across the family room, I noticed how restless he, too, looked, from more than sleep deprivation.

"I thought the baby blues were only supposed to last a couple weeks," he said, voice soft with concern and maybe disappointment, unless that was only my psyche clouding things. I recognized the logical, unspoken next statement: If it lasts longer than the baby blues, it must be post-partum depression. Yes, of course, I'd be the cause of both our unrest. He glanced at me and whispered, "Right?"

I pretended not to hear him, another form of shunning my own reflection. I walked the long way around to the dining room table, through the entryway and living room, before plunking down next to the high chair that waited, like me, in its dust-bunnied corner for Aria to reach solid food age. Or at least head-supporting age. Any day now. I folded my hands on the table's second-hand wood, inhaling to try to erase Abel's observation. He kept his own countdown, apparently: *How long until Mommy's her old self again? Or a reconciliation of her old self and new role. Any day now?* Bad enough how obvious I'd become to him, worse than all those strangers who'd stared at my pregnant belly, remarked about it (or wanted to but knew not to risk a faux pas), and on a couple of occasions had the impudence to rub it.

I glanced at the balloon overhead. Air had seeped from it with painstaking slowness, deepening its crinkles. Strange how something that used to swell and take up so much space, once hollowed, could attract more attention with the depressions that formed. My neck prickled. I scooted the chair back and fled, completing my circuit around the great room through the kitchen, past the pile of baby gifts we weren't ready for yet.

Having rejoined Abel and Aria, I tried to focus on what to get him for his first Father's Day this month. Not a balloon. I got distracted watching him nibble her tiny, puffy cheek. He was such a natural! It left me thinking, *I am not how a mother is supposed to be. Not how I'd envisioned myself lo these many pregnant months. Not how my daughter deserves.*

What have I gotten myself into?

****

That night, while Aria grunted with infant slumber in her bassinet and Abel snored lightly with his back to me, I slid from the bed and crept down to the family room couch in the dark.

An irksome habit throughout my pregnancy of waking around midnight, wresting myself from the serpentine body pillow, flopping off the bed, and shuffling through the dark hallway, down the stairs to the family room couch, had rendered me fearless in our darkened house. My feet knew the path, and now I didn't have to protect my swollen belly from obstacles. I'd learned to ignore the tiny green lights from the emergency flashlight in the bathroom and the outlet near the toaster, not to mention the ghostly beams from the two skylights over the couch. While pregnant, I'd often finished sleeping on my side down there with throw pillows wedged under my belly, my head resting on the sofa arm. Nowadays, I lay on my back in that same spot since I could finally reclaim that position. Of course, I'd grown so out of the habit of back-sleeping, I did it more out of principle than preference.

But tonight, a strange rustling forced my eyes open. It came from a distant corner of the house, the dining room perhaps. Then silence. Probably just ice cubes settling in the freezer behind me. Maybe. I closed my eyes again. Then more rustling, not ice, definitely not from the kitchen. Closer, though. The living room. I watched the corner where the entryway provided the only separation between here and *that sound*.

A bodiless head appeared, hovering above the entry table, catching a hint of light. My heart raced. Not a head, no. That awful balloon. It moved too smoothly to be human. Glided. In diagonals. Just air currents from the heating and cooling vents, I told myself, the throw pillow squashed in my grip. Just a balloon with enough helium to float but not enough to float high anymore.

But it swooped and bobbed slowly toward me, rounding the corner into the family room with too much intentionality, a head without body or face.

I sat up. In a flash, I recalled my stew of emotions when Aria's gaze had first locked onto mine. She was minutes old. They'd laid her on my chest, and those little eyes had peeled open and fixed me with a look I could only peg as disapproving. This was to be our bonding moment, yet all I could think was that single thought that had become a chorus ever since, churning deep inside my flabby stomach each time the words echoed through me: *What have I gotten myself into?*

I stood to face the balloon, my bare feet sweating against the cold floor.

The balloon dipped and slithered toward me like a cobra with head raised, white ribbon trailing across the hardwood floor with a quick, soft swish. I made to move away, but the balloon shot up and wrapped its ribbon around my neck once, twice, squeezing tighter, tiny ridges digging into my skin. I tried to pry my fingers beneath it, but no space, no air! My eyes burned with tears as the balloon turned its plain side to my face, that blank and hideous side, and how could something be both blank and hideous, I didn't know, but it was. The crumpled, reflective surface laid bare all the horrors of a mirror viewed in near-darkness when the mind wrongly fills in the blanks. Like playing Bloody Mary. Blood. Yes, blood streaming from me in the hospital's maternity triage room, down my legs, onto the papery slippers and glossy floor. Later, coating the slimy creature caught from me. So tiny. So consequential. I guess I'd tried to blank those moments from my mind but couldn't. Because I needed them. They marked the moment *I* was so fiercely, irreplaceably needed.

I grabbed it — the balloon, I hoped, not the mirage of my child, though I could no longer tell — hugged it, squeezed it. Crushed it against my belly until my arms, which could now hoist a growing infant for hours on end, shook from its resistance. Finally, the remaining air sighed out of it. The ribbon finally released my neck, and I blacked out.

****

"Candace…"

Abel's voice had never sounded so soft while yelling. Not in the tender sense. The muted sense, as if one of us were trapped in a jar. He repeated my name, and it took me a moment to detect how frantic his faraway cries sounded. I forced my eyes open. He was gripping my hands and stooping over me, bellowing. As soon as he realized I'd come to, he helped me to my feet.

"I heard a bang and came running," he said. "You must've hit the floor hard. Sweetie, what happened?"

I spied the flattened balloon on the floor, limp and placental. I picked it up and took it straight to the bathroom with the diaper garbage and stuffed it down there, where waste belongs. Then I leaned against the changing table. That boxy, bulky piece of furniture took up so much room in our home, like the baby gates and the high chair, crowding our life. But not forever. My fingertips rested on a pack of diapers. Some things that come out of us must be discarded. They deserve it, like waste or self-doubt. Not my precious Aria.

Abel appeared in the doorway, holding her. Her tiny head bobbed, striving to hold itself up, each nod affirming she wouldn't always need my support. She was the most beautiful creature I'd ever seen. I repeated the thought, making it truer and truer, with three exclamation points. What had I gotten myself into? This: I had the capacity to love in the way I wished. I just needed to reinflate it... Right?

The End

The New Bride by Matthew Wilson

I do not like my new wife
Though Dad wants me to call her dear
Whose teeth pinch when she kisses me
And beneath her hats a pointy ear.

Father says this is for peace
Our two kingdoms to become one
But my new bride is white as milk
And only wakes at the death of the sun.

I am most terrified of bedtime
Though her eyes are filled with charms
But her kisses bite and bleed me
And I shiver in her freezing arms.

Thousands died in the vampire war
And I must do as my king said
But my new bride has no reflection
And spitting vipers on her head.

Queen of Sheba by Todd Hanks

Queen of Sheba, wife of Solomon,
there are many different tales of you.
Founder of nations, mother, and

in other legends demon lover with
a hairy leg and cloven foot.
You are a lady of history draped
in mystery, no known origin or name.

Sheba, your husband was a sorcerer
of dark arts, raising demons from
fiery depths. Were you one of those?

Night Gallery

Honor among Thieves

Review by the late Tom Johnson

- ➢ Title: Honor among Thieves (Historical Adventure)
- ➢ Author: J.M. Aucoin
- ➢ Genre: Historical Adventure
- ➢ ISBN: #978-151272379
- ➢ Price: $12.54; 378 pages
- ➢ Available at: Amazon, Barnes & Nobles, and Thriftbooks.
- ➢ Rating: 5 Stars

"Swashbuckling Adventure at Its Best."

Set in 1609 France, after the religious wars, ex-soldier Darion Delerue de Tarbes now rides with Captain Jaspart de Tremear and his Falcon Highwaymen, seeking coin and adventure. Men of courage and horsemanship are quick with a blade of steel or pistol; the action never lets up. Darion is thrown into a fight that could impel France into another war. Will he end with honor or go down in defeat as a rogue bandit?

This was a rollicking good read, with lots of sword action. The author did his research on seventeenth-century France. His writing puts the reader into the romantic tale of political intrigue, as well as personal honor. Except for the profanity, this novel could have been published in *Argosy* or *Adventure* in the days of pulp magazine thrills and stood beside the classics like *The Three Musketeers*. For me, the profanity was the only mark against this well-written action yarn. I read to escape the world and its faults, and that includes the wide use of profanity in today's literature. Other than this drawback, I highly recommend this swashbuckling adventure to all fans of the genre.

Tom Johnson, Author of *Pangaea: Eden's Planet*

Looks That Kill

Review by the late Tom Johnson

- ➢ Title: Looks That Kill (Murder Mystery)
- ➢ Author: Walter B. Gibson
- ➢ Genre: Murder Mystery
- ➢ ISBN: 978-1514614945
- ➢ Price: $14.95; 237 pages
- ➢ Available at: Amazon, Barnes & Noble, and Thriftbooks
- ➢ Rating: 5 Stars

"A Good Mystery with a Nice Twist."

Valdor the Mighty Mind does his mental magic on the air. Sponsored by Moonbeam Soap Company, the program airs from Studio G between 9:00 and 9:30 p.m. on Tuesday evenings. Visitors leave questions in a box outside the studio door, and the mental wizard tunes in on the visitors' thoughts. One night, a visitor is murdered with an invisible knife in his back. The knife isn't truly invisible; it's made from volcanic rock which is like glass. D.A. Investigator James Dorrance believes someone at the studio is the murderer. A young blonde in the studio had caused an interruption in the program, bringing her in contact with Valdor and the investigation. This also involves them both in the investigation. The big question is if Valdor can read minds, does he know who the murderer is?

This was a fun mystery by magician and *The Shadow* creator, Walter B. Gibson, and you can see the influence in both the character and magic. I wasn't sure who the main character was at times, whether Valdor the Mighty Mind or James Dorrance, the D.A. investigator, but that's in keeping with *The Shadow* novels, in which secondary characters lead the story while the hero stays in the background. But Valdor does not always stay in the background, as, like *The Shadow*, he has to come to the rescue of the blonde, Arlene Jennings, a few times. Definitely a fun read. Highly recommended.

Tom Johnson, Author of *Detective Mystery Stories*

Hathor Legacy: Outcast

Review by the late Tom Johnson

- ➤ Title: Hathor Legacy: Outcast
- ➤ Author: Deborah Bailey
- ➤ Genre: SF/Romance/Mystery
- ➤ ISBN: 978-0984292653
- ➤ Price: $11.97; 272 pages
- ➤ Available at: Amazon, Barnes & Noble, and Apple Books
- ➤ Rating: 5 Stars

"A Fast-Paced Thrill Ride."

Earth's astronomers discovered Hathor in 2224, and soon after, families settled on the new planet. Now, on Hathor, the Guardians are responsible for security of the planet. They are the descendants of the original settlers: the original seven families who were selected from the different lands on Earth. The descendants of the first settlers were discovered to have extrasensory perception and other abilities. When children with special powers are discovered, they are taken and trained to be Guardians. They can kinetically throw powerful blasts of energy, as well as "read" people's emotions – this perhaps through a form of telepathy.

Nadira was taken from her mother at age eight to be trained by her mentor, Zina, her mother's cousin. Now Nadira's power is stronger than most of the others. Only Zina may be more powerful. A robbery at the Demeter Mines on Astarte occurs, and Brandon Keel, the CEO, disappears. His son Jonathan Keel comes to Hathor searching for him. Nadira is ordered to follow Jon in case he contacts another suspect, Ilana Travac. A simple case, perhaps, of just a robbery in a mine, with the usual suspects, but things quickly turn deadly for both Jonathan and Nadira. She is honor-bound to protect Jon, but that doesn't mean falling in love with him. After all, Guardians are only supposed to connect with other Guardians, not other-worlders.

With Zina on their trail, Nadira searches for Ilana Travac, hoping to clear Jonathan of involvement in the robbery. And now, she must even question the involvement of Zina. Does her mentor have something to hide?

This is advertised as a science fiction and interracial romance novel. However, the romance is light, and the difference in race is hardly detectable – as it should be. It is pure science fiction, with lots of action and adventure. Although the plot at first seems simple, it eventually becomes more complicated. Yet, it is the characters that drive the plot. Nadira and Jonathan lead us on a fast-paced thrill ride from page one. The author's voice is clear, and the prose is descriptive. As the below interchange between two main characters show:

He strolled over to take in the Nova City skyline, where silver, gold and jewel-tone spires glistened against the darkened sky.

"Overwhelming, isn't it?"

The whole novel is overwhelming, to be precise. I fell in love with the characters immediately, and they never let me down. Oh, Jonathan does appear to be a spoiled brat at first, and women swoon over him, but Nadira brings out the best in him before the story concludes. If you like science fiction, action, and adventure, you will love *Hathor Legacy*. Highly recommended.

Tom Johnson, Author of *Worlds of Tomorrow*

The Bottom of Your Heart

Review by the late Tom Johnson

- ➤ Title: The Bottom of Your Heart
- ➤ Author: Maurizio de Giovanni
- ➤ Genre: Murder Mystery
- ➤ ISBN: 9781609452940
- ➤ Price: $18.00; 456 Pages
- ➤ Available at: Amazon, Barnes & Noble, and Scribd
- ➤ Rating: 5 Stars

Professor Tullio Lovine del Castello, chair of gynecology at the university, suddenly dives out the topmost window of his office building, but the investigation reveals that he didn't jump; somebody threw him. Someone who is big and strong enough to physically throw him through a window. Now it's up to Commissario Ricciardi and Brigadier Maione to discover who the murderer is. The trail leads to several suspects, a gangster known as the Wolf, a huge and strong man, whose wife died at the hands of the doctor during childbirth; he had vowed to kill the professor. Another suspect is the son of a competing doctor; also, a huge, strong man. The professor had wronged them, and there was a letter of warning from the father. Yet, to prove either is the murderer, it will be a hard case of unraveling real evidence to prove which one.

This was another fantastic trail of crime in 1930s Naples, by the chief investigator cursed with "sight" that reveals the final moments of the victim and their last words. Although those words don't point to the murderer, they do reveal final thoughts, and Commissario Ricciardi must ponder their meaning while speaking with witnesses and suspects in the case. The characters capture the reader from the start and take them on the journey to find the answer to the riddle. Personally, I think this is the best series coming out of Italy. I love the characters, and the writing of Maurizio de Giovanni, and have enjoyed every novel by this fine author so far. Highly recommended for mystery lovers.

Tom Johnson, Author of *Detective Mystery Stories*

Electric Dreams: Seven Futuristic Tales

Review by the late Tom Johnson

- ➢ Title: Electric Dreams
- ➢ Author: Deborah A. Bailey
- ➢ Genre: Science Fiction
- ➢ ISBN: 978-0984292660
- ➢ Price: $7.97; 140 Pages
- ➢ Available at: Amazon, Barnes & Noble, and Kobo
- ➢ Rating: 5 Stars

"A Feel of The Twilight Zone."

This collection contains seven interesting tales of the future: 1) "On the Beach" 2) "Between the Mirror and the Heart" 3) "Electric Schemes" 4) "Stranger in town" 5) "When Words Leave Off" 6) "Roots of Deception" and 7) "A Place in the World."

"On the Beach" features a lone woman on a space station. Her only companions are computers, and they're slowly taking over all systems. She thinks about the beach and how nice it would be there among people, when she suddenly hears voices. Children's laughter. She can only question the computer if she is going crazy.

"Between the Mirror and the Heart" was my favorite story. A human woman purchases a *Companion,* a male robot named Kyle. But problems arise when she discovers she is in love with him. Leaving him alone, she travels to another planet on her job, perhaps to put him behind her and find human companionship. While she's away, Kyle meets another *Companion,* and when her human becomes ill, and she must leave, Kyle invites her to stay with him. Will this complicate things?

"Electric Schemes" follows an office worker and his computer. He's being taken advantage of by his boss, and the computer doesn't like it.

"Stranger in Town" is more of an urban fantasy, about a woman who lives in poverty until she meets a stranger who offers her marriage and a future. But he's somewhere far off, and she's waiting for his return, and the fulfillment of the promise. A good story.

"When Words Leave Off" is really part of the same universe that we find in the following two stories. Lt. Commander Tasha Grant and Benjamine Tragg are researching language encryption and it is time to present their study to the Commodore and visiting professors. They are on the ship Marlo above the planet Demeter, where Fleet Base Three is located. Meantime, Tasha is preparing for a concert, and time is pressing. I really like what the author says in

Tasha's voice: "Even if I hadn't won, it was worth it to have competed. It's not about being judged, it's about being confident in who you are and what you can do."

In "Roots of Deception," Akida Shera, the Kuhani and Kasi (religious leader) of the planet Tulluran, must help her people rebuild their civilization after the Kellian occupation. The Terrans have set up Fleet Base Three on Demeter, and offer protection against the Kellians or any other invaders, but things are not as simple as all that.

"A Place in the World" still follows Sheras Kuhani, the Kasi religious leader, as she must maintain control of her world, even if it means challenging the governing body and the Commodore on Demeter for power. There is much division between the people on the subject of the Terrans having power on their world.

These were all interesting yarns, with a touch of the *Twilight Zone* in a few, while the last three stories introduce us to the beginnings of the Hathor series. The planet Demeter will also be in that universe. But take each of the seven stories for their own brief read for what they are, science fiction from the mind of a fan. I think readers will enjoy them. I know I did. Highly recommended.

Tom Johnson, Author of *These Alien Skies*

Gone Missing

Review by the late Tom Johnson

- ➤ Title: Gone Missing
- ➤ Author: Camy Tang
- ➤ Genre: Inspirational Romance/Suspense
- ➤ ISBN: 978- 0373676798
- ➤ Price: $5.22; 281 Pages (Large Print)
- ➤ Available at: Amazon, Thriftbooks, and Google Books
- ➤ Rating: 5 Stars

"Fast-Paced, Thrill-A-Minute Action."

Receiving a postcard from her friend, Fiona, who is in trouble and needs help, Joslyn Dimalanta decides to go look for her. In training as a skip tracer, she can track Fiona's movements. But others are looking for Fiona too, and to make matters worse, Fiona's half-brother Clay Ashton joins up with her, and his good looks just might capture Joslyn's heart.

This was light on romance and heavy on action and suspense, but the writer doesn't preach to her readers. Yet her writing clearly shows her faith, and she's not afraid to throw a punch. You don't have to be a Christian to read her novels, but you will admire her for her personal stand and her ability to tell an exciting yarn. Highly recommended.

Tom Johnson, Author of *Detective Mystery Stories*

48

Winter's Vampire
by
Marge Simon

There's a vampire for every season, a little-known fact. The cruelest of them all belongs to Winter. While the bites of others convey a warm death to their victims, Winter's vampire only metes out doom. Her deadly kiss freezes the mind with fear and all who gaze upon their corpse are damned to waking nightmares. It is well for humankind that Winter's Vampire enjoys winter sports. Thus, if you stay free of ski lodges, hockey games, and ice-skating rinks, the chances of being drained by Winter's Vampire are slim. But bear in mind there are other seasons, other sports, and other vampires.

Treasure
by
Sandy DeLuca

Denim, size five, circa 1970s, trimmed with beads, lace, a bit of velvet. An eccentric time machine, in a thrift shop on Elm, retro clothes on mannequins in the front window, good prices on housewares, silver tag sales on Fridays. Old women, the less fortunate, and an occasional collector will go inside. I shop there for old china and teacups, but last week, draped over a bohemian style quilt, laid a pair of bell bottoms — exactly like a pair I owned back in the day. I wore them when I rehearsed for a part in Jesus Christ Superstar … Magdalene. The play ran in the summer of 1978, the old opera house in Chelsea. Anna came to every show.

Those jeans, with a price tag a bit too high. Yet, I indulged myself, asking the salesgirl if I could try them on. Perfect fit, nostalgic, Anna smiling at me as I said my lines.   I thanked the clerk and went on my way.

Thursday night, I woke up thinking about those denims, how Anna sewed embellishments … to sleeves, necklines, to blue jeans; needle and thread, thimble on her thumb, materials we found in my grandma's attic. Oh, how I loved Anna's delicate fingers, mercurial, lovely.

Those days, smoky autumn, laughing together about boys we'd met, about the future. She'd be a dress designer and I'd be an actress. And she'd sew while I recited Shakespeare. Cloth and words, twining and raveling apart. Dreams shared with my best friend, gone so long. I had few reminders of her, so I had to buy those pants. It was her work … I knew it. But would they still be there?

Opening time is 9:00 a.m. I was there two minutes before, holding my breath, sighing as the girl flicked on the lights, revealing my treasure … still there. I made the purchase, using the last of my weekly paycheck.

Once home, I hung the nostalgic pair in my closet, mesmerized by sparkling beads, by the way lace and velvet made perfect patterns. I thought about Anna working into the night. Cradling the masterpiece in her arms, flinching when a drop of blood trickled from her flesh, her eyes wide when I sang to her. Magic ritual, performed on a moonlit night.

And, for a while, the spells worked … but only for her. So many decades ago, she designed clothes for women who lived in Newport mansions, on her way to New York to design costumes for Broadway shows. I auditioned for all of them, was turned away, while directors and thespians invited her to parties in East Side lofts.

And those hands … Anna's lovely hands … cut material bought in downtown shops, colors, patterns, charms and rhinestones … glowing beneath stage lights. And I went with her to all the parties, feeling awkward when people asked who I was.

"An actress," I'd tell them. And they smiled sympathetically, sizing me up, taking in my plump body, hair a bit too curly, a smile not pretty enough for applauds. No amount of prayer, or sacrifices of bone and flesh, helped me.

I told myself that my time would come, and I didn't cry … didn't purchase the switchblade … until the night she told me I couldn't go along, that people wouldn't understand … that I wasn't part of the crowd.

Anna had been mine before those people took her from me … my friend … a girl who sewed fancy cuffs on a pair of my old blue jeans … while she whispered chants to shadowy gods. And I knew those denims were potent, all her wishes for me meshed within each stitch.

Years later, when I found those pants again, I sat cross-legged in front of my closet, swearing that Anna sat beside me, her hands clasped, tears in her eyes. And she told me, "I'm alone … and so cold. I tried for you. But your heart is dark…"

Sorrow welled up inside me. How could I be so selfish? So, I tore apart the needlework, destroying the beauty, just as I'd destroyed my friendship … my love … for Anna … both our lives. And it all tumbled onto the floor, shimmering gemstones, colorful strands, two delicate phalanges from her thumb.

At sunset, I buried slacks … thread … fabric … bones in a grave behind my barn … Anna's resting place, unmarked, unknown to everyone but me. Wind flurried brown leaves over her plot, covering gifts to a ghostly seamstress … whispering lines from a play no one will see.

The End

Unholy Hungers by Alexis Child

You were burning like fire
With stars in your eyes
Growling like black thunder
Before the deadly battle
With fangs shining

Avenger of the dark

Your lips bled with syrupy scarlet
On pillows stained in blood
As you sank your lips into
Unwilling flesh
Like the rosy snow in a wild dawn

Makes of a mist

On the edge of town
In this ancient graveyard
Clutching a cross in naked hand

Nowhere to hide in a forsaken land

You preyed on the lonely
Making us think we were
Your one and only
Leaving behind holes

Where you sucked out souls

Beg me to put you in the sun
And set you free
Pleasure will never be yours
As your soul purpose is to feed
Eternity calls forth the blood

Of breathless tears

Emotional vampire
There is no cure
For only seeking another's pleasure
Only the moon will remember
The hold you had on us throughout the years
In the winds of time, how blinded

Are we to our fears

She'll take you down slow
You won't even know
Until she releases her hold
Leaving behind only holes
Where she's sucked out souls

She's an emotional vampire
She'll burn you like Hell's fire
A boiling cauldron spilling over
Like a dark cupid Witch
Hell's dark Pope
In evil's cradle
A Demon's kiss

She sparkles like a sapphire
That emotional vampire
She stalks the night
For what she can't put just right
A dark perpetual romance
In the glaring daylight

Haiku One by Denny E. Marshall
Halloween bonus
pumpkins frightening sidekicks
watermelon heads

Manor of Madness
by
Lee Clark Zumpe

The car eased off the smooth asphalt strip that linked Florida's east and west coast, connecting two urban dots on opposite sides of the state and partitioning vast swathes of acreage predominately owned by apathetic corporations and maintained by armies of migrant workers.

A narrow dirt road stretched tidily to the far southern horizon, disappearing beneath the leafy branches of citrus trees.

"How could anyone possibly spot that from the road?" Mildly disgusted, Kathleen Sawyer pitched a tattered folding map into the backseat of the Kia Rio. Largely defaced by veins of pink, yellow, and lime-green highlighter, the 10-year-old document did not record the intersection of State Road 60 and Drunk Mary Road several miles east of Lake Wales. Sitting in the passenger seat, she gazed at a rusty old tin street sign bearing the curious name, fastened to an old wooden utility pole by heavy-duty garden wire. "Wouldn't you think this guy would want to advertise out here or something?"

"Maybe he makes most of his contacts online." Russell Drake had stumbled upon the dealer's posting on an Internet message board. The 52-year-old filmmaker-turned-entrepreneur looked at his passenger, trying to gauge the magnitude of her misgivings. She lacked his sense of adventure. "It's not exactly the kind of place you'd just stop for a quick look around, you know. Not exactly a run-of-the-mill antique store."

The business they sought specialized in the salvage, restoration, and resale of vintage carnival rides. Its owner, "Curly" Keith Barth, boasted that he had amassed hundreds of traditional pieces, which he dutifully refurbished and maintained on his 50-acre spread in central Florida.

As sporadic weekday traffic sped by behind them, the two quietly stared down the long, dusty corridor leading deep into the orange grove, wordlessly wondering if their spur-of-the-moment journey from the mountains of North Carolina had been particularly prudent. Kathleen, especially, questioned her own reckless behavior. She knew that Russell had left no notes about his itinerary, told no one of his intentions. She, meanwhile, had forged a bogus tale about visiting a friend in Jacksonville, withholding the truth from everyone, including her mother and her estranged husband.

Her dishonesty stemmed from her on-again, off-again affair with Russell.

"Russ," Kathleen said, trying to conceal her apprehension, "you checked this guy out with the Better Business Bureau or the local chamber of commerce, didn't you?"

"I checked some of his references," he said, although none of them had bothered to respond to his e-mails. "His licenses checked out with the state, too. He's probably just a little eccentric but in a good, artsy way. Like me."

"You're sure it's worth it?" Kathleen sneered as she asked the question, knowing Russell's tenacity. Once he had settled on an objective, he never relented. Absurdly wealthy people had that luxury when it came to squandering funds on folly and decadent indulgences.

"We haven't even cleared it with the zoning board. They may not let you bring it inside city limits."

"Codes are negotiable, and the board owes me favors for bringing tourists back to Yonah."

Russell had settled in the little North Carolina town after retiring at age 40, a string of wildly successful, straight-to-video horror flicks to his credit. The founder and creative force behind Cinister Cinema, between 1985 and 1997, Russell directed nearly 40 films, including cult classics such as *Crypt Dweller*, *Zombie Plague*, *Feast of the Dead*, *Night of Shed Skin,* and *Witch in the Window*. Having accumulated a vast fortune between royalties and a lucrative franchising scheme, Russell purchased two whole city blocks in economically depressed downtown Yonah and began stockpiling horror movie memorabilia.

A few years later, he opened his *Museum of the Macabre*, featuring revolving exhibits showcasing Hollywood's most recognizable movie monsters.

The museum began drawing crowds, and Russell channeled profits into expanding the business. Within a few years, he had turned Yonah into a mecca for horror connoisseurs, adding a convention center, a genre-specific bookstore, and a theater complex where he established the annual Yonah Horror Film Festival, which attracted both hungry greenhorns and industry veterans.

Never entirely satisfied with his handiwork, Russell had a new brainchild. He wanted to add vintage carnival dark rides to his ever-growing empire. In particular, he sought one that he cited as a source of inspiration for his occupation … an attraction that had so warped his mind with delicious fear during his childhood that he still suffered occasional nightmares spawned by the terrors it housed.

Kathleen, his business manager and intermittent romantic partner, disapproved of his plan. Still as eye-catching as the day he had hired her as his financial advisor, the 35-year-old dealt with the day-to-day drudgery that kept his enterprise afloat, deftly handling the all-technical intricacies and mercantile rituals with a disciplined demeanor connoting a degree of bureaucratic bliss.

She had agreed to accompany him despite her reservations, if only to provide a voice of reason.

The car inched forward in Florida's sandy soil, slipping beneath the arched canopy of emerald leaves and kicking up dust clouds in its wake. The highway disappeared behind them in no time, and the path ahead seemed endless. The lichen-covered trunks of the orange trees pressed inward on either side, crowding the narrow corridor. They both peered down infinite avenues clotted by patchy flourishes of weeds, marveling at the flawlessness of geometry and wondering if the meticulousness of the design bordered on fanaticism.

"If you find what you're looking for," Kathleen said, noticing that the skies had dimmed but unable to see the inevitable storm clouds beginning their daily march toward the Gulf of Mexico, "how will you get it out of here?"

"There must be an alternate route," Russell said, his response coming so quickly that it was obvious the same thought had been rattling through his skull. "I'll be sure to mention it, though. I'm not planning on transporting it back to North Carolina, anyway. If delivery isn't part of the sale, the deal's off."

"Wouldn't it be easier to hire a contractor to design and build a new ride?" Kathleen had already offered Russell several different options, trying to limit the expense of what she considered his riskiest venture to date – particularly during a recession. "That way, you would avoid the hassle of upgrading everything to meet code requirements."

"It wouldn't be the same," Russell said. "It wouldn't be authentic." He sensed her lingering skepticism. While he valued her business acumen and her flair for merchandising, Russell realized that she still did not understand why the museum appealed to so many people. She did not comprehend the allure of horror, the thrill people experienced when immersed in unadulterated fear. "A modern mock-up of one of these rides wouldn't induce the same sense of terror. It wouldn't *feel* scary."

"With today's technology, it would be more realistic, more graphic."

"Maybe," Russell admitted. "But the vintage ride has age on its side."

"What do you mean?"

"Okay, you're standing on a dark street late one night and it starts raining." As Russell described the scenario, oversized raindrops crashed into the windshield. Thunder roared and flashes of lightning danced through the orchard. "On one side of the street, there's an old three-story Victorian house, weedy front lawn, shutters dangling precariously. A couple of newlyweds are living there now, but before they moved in, the place had been empty for at least a decade – ever since the last tenant was found dead in the basement.

"On the other side of the street is a modern single-family home, three bedrooms, two bathrooms, no more than five years old. The lawn needs to be mowed, and the planters need tending. The original owner hanged himself in the garage, but the place sold and is now occupied by a young couple." He paused, letting her digest the essentials. "The storm is getting worse, and you know you need to call a taxi. Lights are on in both windows. Which house do you choose?"

"I use my cell phone," Kathleen said without hesitation. She looked at the rainwater collecting in gullies along the side of the road, felt the car's tires sloshing through mud puddles in the downpour. "But I get your point," she finally said. "You're not selling the ride itself so much as the associated legends with carnival lore."

"Yes," he said, "but it's more than that, too." The windshield wipers worked relentlessly, battling the deluge. The path beneath the orange trees had become a murky passageway, but Russell thought he glimpsed light at the end of the long, leafy tunnel. "The older something like that is – be it a haunted house, abandoned church, medieval castle, or carnival ride – the more likely it is that it has absorbed some of the fear it has generated in the past. Soaking up all those intense emotions reinforces its efficiency."

"That's crazy," Kathleen said. "But it makes for a good sales pitch."

The rain diminished to a steady drizzle as the car emerged from the sprawling orchard, coming to rest on a thin band of earth sparsely populated by pines and palmetto scrub. Just ahead, a dense hammock loomed. At the edge of the forest, the statue of an enormous painted clown stood watch, its fat crimson lips preset in a maniacal grin, its hands tucked behind its back as if concealing some reprehensible gag.

The clown's head tilted to one side menacingly.

An asymmetrical old one-story farmhouse sat not far beyond the sinister-looking jester, rambling beneath the verdant canopy and surrounded by pine straw and creeping tendrils of kudzu. A few neglected rose bushes clustered along the screened veranda and two magnolias – one on either side of the house – with their broad leaves promising to blossom come May.

Away from the modest estate, planned vegetation and pine trees gave way to the more common types of trees found in a Florida hammock, including sweet gum, hickory, palms, holly, and in greatest numbers and glory expansive live oaks. Their spreading limbs were draped with Spanish moss.

Amidst the labyrinth of broad boughs and tangled vines, Russell and Kathleen gradually discerned the graveyard of abandoned carnival rides. In the first instant of discovery, Russell felt an inebriating fusion of wonder, delight, and trepidation. A cobweb of orange power cables spread across the pine straw connecting the facades of various old midway whimsies and threatening a backwoods inferno. Though faded, the bold hues of their brightly painted faces seemed like colors extracted from some other dimension – a reality somewhere beyond space and time.

Along with the fun houses and carousels and bumper cars and zippers, immediately visible were a variety of enticing dark rides with wickedly clever names like Horror House, Screamville, Montresor's Wild Ride, Shoggoth Cavern, Zombie Asylum, and Darkshade Laboratory.

Then, reality surfaced. Battered and neglected, these rusting hulks revealed little evidence of the advertised "restoration," displaying a tragic and terminal collapse and gradual attrition that would eventually make them an indiscernible component of the surrounding environment. Framed by rows of broken bulbs, tarnished by graffiti, and marred by corrosion, their threadbare condition lent credence to Kathleen's prevailing skepticism.

The Kia Rio came to rest on a level patch of manicured Bermuda grass in front of the farmhouse. A tall, wiry man sat on the porch wearing jeans, an unbuttoned short-sleeve flannel shirt, and a baseball cap bearing the bold green collegiate letters "DUI," followed by – in smaller type – "Drunkard's University of Intoxication." He propped his feet up on an old orange cooler.

"You must be that fellow from North Carolina," he said as Russell stretched his legs and climbed out of the car. "Glad you could make it. I'm Curly. Curly Barth."

"Nice to meet you, Curly. I'm Russell Drake." Russell shot Kathleen a disapproving glance as she sat motionless in the passenger seat, eyeing the Floridian with disdain. She didn't try to hide her displeasure at this point, believing the folly of the entire enterprise could be corroborated by the abundant examples of mechanical decrepitude around them. "Not easy finding you out here."

"Yeah, sorry I had to bring you in the back route," Curly said, nodding toward the narrow dirt path they had traveled. "Got a paved drive out to Lake Clinch Road, but the bridge over Clinch Creek washed out last rainy season we had. County won't replace it. I got the money, but it's the principle of the thing." Curly – not yet willing to resign his comfortable chair – took a long sip from a tall glass of iced tea. "No sense standing in the sun, Russ." Russell had been lingering at an open gate in a short, white picket fence that hemmed the farmhouse in from the surrounding wilderness. "Why don't you join me? Bring your lady friend, too."

"Come on, Kathleen," Russell said, looking over his shoulder. She reluctantly opened her door and stepped into the Florida heat. "Kathleen oversees my finances," he told Curly. "She's here to keep me from buying anything I don't need."

"Always pays to have a voice of reason," Curly said, shrugging off his chronic malaise and struggling to his feet. "Let me fetch some more glasses and a pitcher of tea. May as well go over things out here. Ain't no cooler in the house."

****

Curly Barth spent nearly an hour recounting his odd tale – his mother, cast out by her family due to a teenage pregnancy, had joined a traveling circus that wintered in Florida. Carnival workers had raised him; he learned every job along the way from concessionaire and ride supervisor to barker and accountant. He knew the rides intimately, from set-up to break-down and every on-the-spot mechanical repair imaginable.

"Hold on just a minute," Curly said, excusing himself as he disappeared into the house. He returned with a shoebox filled with old Polaroid photos, a history of the carnival in one-of-a-kind snapshots. "That's Mama and me and Alex the Albino," Curly said, pointing at one of the images as he handed the box to Russell.

"These are incredible," Russell said, flipping through the pictures.

"Mama and me, we took over that circus from the previous owners right around 1945 – I'd just turned 18," Curly said. Russell did the math. He found it difficult to believe that Curly could be in his 80s. Until that moment, Russell thought they were about the same age. "Mama saw to it that everything was put in my name, said that was to make up for all the years she couldn't afford no birthday presents."

"How long did you keep the show going?"

"More than 25 years," Curly said. "Made piles of money, too. That was back in the heyday, the 50s and the 60s." Curly's wistfulness grew more noticeable as he watched Russell study the box of photographs. "Brought a lot of those folks back with me when I settled here … built them cottages out in the woods. They're all gone now, all passed. Nothing left but me and the rides."

"Which brings us back to the reason for our visit," Kathleen interjected, eager to get back to business. "I was noticing that a lot of the equipment outside isn't in pristine condition, as advertised."

"Kathleen, that's a bit harsh, isn't it?" Russell smiled to hide his momentary embarrassment.

"No, the lady has a valid point," Curly said. "Thing is, the exterior is the last thing I worry about out here. That's the easiest part to clean up. I concentrate first on rebuilding the machinery and refurbishing the interior. Some of these rides show up all hollowed out, all their guts picked clean. That's where I do my best work."

"So, you get them up and running first," Russell said, "before you bother with the façade. Makes sense." He shot Kathleen a holier-than-thou glance as if he had won an unspoken bet. "And how about the one I'm interested in? How about Manor of Madness?"

"Oh, she was in fine shape when I took her in," Curly said. "That old girl stands up to time and nature. She don't show her age one bit." He stood abruptly, beckoning them. "Come on, ya'll. Let's take a ride."

A few minutes later, the ranch-style farmhouse disappeared as Curly led his potential customers on a trek through the Florida wilderness, weaving through the eerily serene collection of carnival relics. When the old Manor of Madness attraction appeared, Russell felt a weird blend of anxiety, excitement, titillation, trauma, and nausea.

"Climb aboard," Curly said, offering Kathleen a hand as she stepped forward, but she politely declined his assistance. Russell took the first available car, eager for the opportunity to revisit his childhood. Each black, spinning, high-back car – reminiscent of those built by the Pretzel Amusement Ride Company – had been embellished with a gruesome, hand-sculpted human skull cradled by willowy tentacles. "I guess I don't need to tell ya'll to keep your arms and legs inside the vehicle."

"How long is it?" Kathleen asked.

"Oh, I'd say there's roughly 950 feet of track," Curly said. By her vexed expression, he realized she was more interested in the duration of the ride. "Shouldn't take you no more than three minutes, long as there's no mechanical problems." Curly sauntered over to the control console. He flipped a couple of toggle switches before punching the large, red button that would send the riders on their way. "Have fun, now."

Russell's car jerked forward on the single-rail track, staggering a little at first, then smoothly advancing toward a vaulted doorway. The doors abruptly swung wide, revealing a shadowed antechamber inhabited by a grim undertaker clutching a measuring tape. His stony gaze had potentially sized up thousands of passersby, offering a silent vow to have a coffin waiting should they not survive the encounter.

The funerary motif continued as the tight, twisting, turning track proceeded around a tight curve, entering a parlor where a vintage, working Charm'in Charles greeted him, its boney fingers hovering over the square piano's keys. Russell recognized the skeleton playing the upright as one manufactured and marketed by Funni-Frite, a gag that had once served as a fashionable centerpiece in the dark ride industry of the 1960s. Russell felt its placement in this ride misled riders – insinuating familiarity and predictability.

The car next burst through a series of crash-through doors disguised as flagstone walls. A complete absence of music and sound effects suggested audio problems; but, as the car entered the next chamber, Russell heard the muted howl of strong winds carrying a most peculiar tune played by some mad flutist.

"Still with me," Russell said as his car spun around for the first time, bringing him face-to-face with Kathleen, seated in the car behind him. "Pretty neat, huh?"

"No one will pay to see this," she said before disappearing in shadow.

Russell's car next traversed what appeared to be a common revolving barrel stunt, its interior adorned with luminous stars that appeared to march across the firmament. The vivid illusion, meant to disorient the rider, fascinated Russell. He could not grasp how the design-ers made it appear as though dark figures squatted in the depths of the faux cosmos.

Next, he found himself gliding down a narrow aisle of bookshelves in the manor's library. Though he had not noticed the names of the tomes displayed as a child, the visible titles of the collected works surprised him. Among the volumes, he spotted copies of *Cultes des Goules, Magiae naturalis, Unaussprechlichen Kulten, Welt von Schatten, Andere Götter, De Vermis Mysteriis, Culto Cattivo,* and *Conversations avec les morts.*

Passing through a patch of utter darkness that somehow reproduced the barrenness and chill of deep space, Russell found himself traversing a room filled with cockeyed timber supports and strangely skewed walls. Coupled with the eerie lighting, the overall effect challenged the mind's ability to calculate the chamber's perimeter. The uncanny geometry of the surroundings alone evoked a stimulating sense of dread.

An oversized rodent with a curiously human face stood defiantly on its hind legs while scratching arcane symbols across the woodwork. Unlike the cheesy Charm'in Charles and the tacky undertaker, this unsettling mock-up possessed disturbingly convincing features and sophisticated, albeit primitive, animatronics. Mesmerized by the perverse creature, Russell nearly leapt out of his seat when he felt the sudden sweep of rats swarming over his shoes and brushing his pant legs. Looking down, he saw nothing.

The ritual room followed. Russell slowly approached a group of five hooded figures encircling an altar. Artificial candlelight bathed the chamber in a dull glow, revealing both the pedestrian pentagram and magic circle as well as more elaborate, eccentric symbols of the black arts. The faceless disciples chanted as they went about their work mechanically, their victim primarily concealed in shadow.

As the blade completed its initial incision, the woman's screams filled the room. Strategic lighting illuminated the stream of blood pouring over the side of the table while the victim's legs – amazingly lifelike – kicked and twitched. Details included pink toenails and a small rose tattoo just above her right ankle.

Russell tensed as one of the figures spun around on his heels, clutching an all-too-realistic beating heart.

The high-back car stopped abruptly, and Russell found himself staring down into an impossibly deep pit lit by distant emerald fires. The conjurer drew back his hood exposing an artificial countenance that seemed to mask something far more hideous, yet unquestionably natural.

"Child of the darkness, you have propagated fear and madness through your endeavors." Russell, startled by unexpected paralysis, had no recollection of this part of the ride. Still, the voice sounded familiar. "As ever, we are indebted to you. Now, we ask you to bring us fresh souls that we may torture them in the fields of nightmare."

The conjurer smiled, relaxing his grip on the bloody heart until it tumbled down into the pit. He and the other disciples stepped aside, and Russell glared at the corpse splayed over the stone altar. Before he could react, before he could give voice to his anger or suppress his sickness, he felt the car tilting forward, forcing him first to stare down into the realm of horrors hidden within the confines of the carnival ride.

He lurched forward in the seat, numb fingers ineffectually clawing at the guard rail, as he spilled out of the car. Helplessly he fell, reeling until he found himself kneeling on a rocky promontory overlooking a gray wasteland spread beneath a vast black canopy. The sky featured a central ravenous vortex that fed mercilessly upon surrounding galaxies. Volcanoes dotted the horizon, belching soot and heaving cascades of green lava.

Russell recognized thousands of ill-fated carnival-goers populating the unspeakable dominion, intercepted and interned over the decades. Forced to endure appalling, indescribable torment and suffering dependent on the whims of nameless, callous gods, most of the enslaved denizens had decomposed, though death had never freed them from their ordeal.

The awful resonance of their combined cries infested Russell's mind, threatening to spark insanity. As the prospect of madness passed, however, Russell realized he had heard the dreadful cacophony once before – on his last visit to the Manor of Madness. It was the memory of that terrible clamor that had inspired him.

Russell closed his eyes and waited for the ride to resume.

****

YONAH – The grand opening of Manor of Madness, a new exhibit at Russell Drake's Museum of Madness, took place Oct. 29.

Participating in the event were several members of local government, including Yonah's new mayor and the president and vice-president of the Yonah Chamber of Commerce. Joining in the ceremony were several horror industry representatives, including well-known authors and filmmakers.

Drake, founder of Cinister Cinema, said in a press release that this would be the first of several fun houses and carnival rides he plans to bring to the town. Proceeds from the opening day festivities will benefit the Search for Kathleen Sawyer Foundation. Sawyer, Drake's former business advisor, was reported missing last year while visiting family in Florida.
"I hope that Manor of Madness brings plenty of business to Yonah," Drake went on to say in the press release. "I hope that it serves to inspire a mix of creativity and terror in those who dare to ride it." *Yonah Centennial Beacon*

The End

Darkedge by Lee Clark Zumpe

I remember being a blade once,
A promise of victory;
A harvester of death;
The object of a curse
Upon a warrior's breath.

I cut the air at his command,
I shimmered in the sun.
I slept in leathern bed;
And on days of battle
I was bathed in red.

A name I know he gave to me:
I, a brother he trusted,
I, his only real friend;
Darkedge is what he called me
Till he met his tragic end.

With grace I saw years pass by,
My thirst was yet unquenched,
And still my bite was keen;
But the warrior used me little
For he was not what he had been.

When finally, he roused me from my sleep,
Face withered, eyes distant,
He simply wanted to rest;
I wept for the warrior's youth
As I plunged into his breast.

The Soporific Pillows of Pan
by
Hillary Lyon

Devon slit the packing tape with his pocket knife and pried open the cardboard box. Inside were two pillows, each in a green plastic shipping bag.

"Uh, thanks?"

"Honey—you've been complaining about not getting a good night's sleep for, like, ages," Naomi said as she sidled up close to him. "And this pillow has, like, over *two thousand* five-star reviews on the shopping website! 'Improve the Quality of Your Life with Pan's Soporific Pillows: For a Sleep Fathoms Deep.'" She closed her eyes as she recited the ad's line.

Naomi suddenly hugged him and swayed. "So I thought this would be just the thing for you."

"I suppose the other one is for you?" Devon asked as Naomi's motives were rarely so generous.

She giggled. "Of course!" Naomi broke her hug to look Devon in the eye. "They were having a sale, like you get two pillows for the price of—"

"Okay," Devon smiled. She could be selfish, but she was a thrifty shopper.

Naomi grabbed one of the green plastic bags and tore it open. She pulled the pillow out and squeezed it. "Just feel this! It's fluffy, yet firm, *exactly* like the advertisement says. How cool is that?"

Devon opened the remaining bag and squeezed that pillow. It was true! The pillow was very fluffy, yet somehow also firm. Maybe there was something to this.

"Oh, and speaking of cool," Naomi said as she held the pillow up to her cheek, "these babies are supposed to stay cool under your head *all* night long. Even during summertime—when *somebody* keeps the air conditioner's thermostat cranked up to save money."

Devon laughed. The thermostat setting was an ongoing petty battle between them, a veritable war of one or two degrees. It had become a joke. "Okay, let's try them out tonight."

"Awesome! You're gonna get the best night's sleep *ever*," Naomi said as she danced away. "You can thank me in the morning."

****

The next morning, Devon woke up refreshed, though he had a stiff neck. *Suppose that's from sleeping on a new pillow,* he reasoned. *I'll get used to it.*

"Hey, good morning, handsome," Naomi squeaked when she joined him in the bathroom. As she squeezed toothpaste onto her brush, she nodded to his reflection in the mirror. She raised an eyebrow.

He rinsed the shaving cream off his razor. "What?"

"I don't recall getting busy last night," she tittered. Her eyes sparkled. "Though I did have some intense dreams—got some serious REM sleep, I guess, but—" she pointed to the side of his neck with the handle of her toothbrush, "did I do that?"

Devon lifted his head to examine the side of his throat in the mirror. A hickey! *Jeez,* he snorted to himself, *how high school romance.* "Well, if *you* didn't, I don't know who did." He was more than a little annoyed; this would be impossible to hide from his coworkers; it wasn't difficult for him to imagine the ribbing he would get at the office. Maybe he could use some of Naomi's makeup to disguise this embarrassing love token.

As if she'd read his mind, she opened her makeup drawer and pawed through it before handing him a tube of concealer. "You know the guys in your department will be *jealous*." She happily sang out that last word as she left the bathroom.

After more than a week, the hickey faded. No one at work noticed; if they did, they had the courtesy not to mention it.

****

Devon threw his keys into the bowl on the small table by the front door. They clanked harshly, announcing his arrival home.

Naomi stuck her head out of the kitchen doorway. "Somebody's home early! I thought I'd make Neapolitan pizza for dinner to surprise you—but now there's no surprise." She pursed her lips in an exaggerated pout, which usually made him laugh.

But not tonight; he was too tired to laugh. "Man, what a day," Devon said as he shrugged off his jacket. "I'm sorry, babe—I'm not all that hungry." He flopped down on the couch. "I just want to go to bed."

Naomi scampered over to him, wiping her hands on a dishtowel. "I hope you're not getting sick." She felt his forehead. "Your skin is cool, if anything. Not hot." She walked back towards the kitchen. "Why don't you go on to bed if you're *that* beat? We can always eat this yummy pie tomorrow."

Devon could hear the disappointment in her voice, but he was too exhausted to care. "Okay, thanks," he mumbled as he struggled to raise himself from the couch. The idea of climbing the stairs to their bedroom was daunting. He supposed he could sleep here on the couch, but—he really wanted to nestle his head on his fluffy-yet-firm pillow.

He imagined the pillow on his side of the bed, waiting for him. It was always cool, and invited him to rest his work-weary head and dream an uninhibited, kaleidoscopic dream. He *needed* to lie his head on the soft cloud of that pillow; a need which was akin to debilitating thirst, to ravenous hunger.

He trudged up the stairs.

****

He was out as soon as his head hit that pillow.

The women in his dreams were nymphs, he ascertained, as their smooth skin was a pale green, their long, tangled hair various shades of brown, the color of their eyes ranged from glittering emerald green to shining gold. Every night, several of these creatures nimbly tiptoed over to him and surrounded him. They affectionately stroked his arms, they cooed sweet love words into his hair, they ardently kissed his neck and chest—

Increasingly, those kisses stung, though not enough to wake him. Still, they left marks— those embarrassing reddish-purple hickeys. *Love-bites* the nymphs called them. Devon had become adept at hiding these marks with concealer, with his clothes artfully arranged. He'd even been able to conceal them from Naomi. If she noticed, she didn't comment. Perhaps she had grown as tired of him as he was of her. Perhaps she also experienced her own erotic romps in dreamland; maybe she played with seductive satyrs.

It's not cheating, he reassured himself, *if it takes place in dreams.*

Increasingly, he awoke sated but fatigued. A truly good night's sleep was something he hadn't experienced in weeks—but he was not about to sacrifice his dream-time playmates for a deep sleep, no matter how refreshed he'd feel in the morning. His phantasmagorical Saturnalias were too delicious, too satisfying; he didn't just want to experience them—he *needed* to experience them.

****

Monday morning, Devon dragged himself out of bed to prepare for the work day. His reflection in the bathroom mirror showed him a gray-skinned, gaunt-faced man, with cheeks and chin bedecked with stubble and dark shadows beneath his haunted eyes. His shoulders sagged; he was too tired to shave, much less brush his teeth. He'd chew gum in his car on the way to work.

Naomi slid past him to get to her sink. She caught his bloodshot eye in the mirror. "Good heavens, you look peaked," she said in her motherly voice. "Maybe you should call in sick, spend the day in bed." Before he could answer, she turned back to the mirror, engrossed in applying her mascara.

You're obviously sleeping well, Devon thought as he watched her put on her makeup. *Rosy cheeks, bright eyes, and you're bursting with all-natural, uncaffeinated energy. Since when are you a morning person?*

She parted her lips and ran her tongue across her teeth. "You know, I don't seem to need as much sleep as I used to—I suppose I am getting such high-quality slumber with that new pillow, that my metabolism is more efficient." She turned to him and playfully opened his bathrobe. Her fingers lightly touched each hickey on his neck and chest before she pressed down—*hard*—on the biggest one over his heart. Prickly needles of electricity radiated from that token; blinding sparks burst in the backs of his eyes. He jerked back, away from her finger.

"Ouch!" he whined. "That hurt."

"Oh, please," Naomi scoffed as she moved out of the bathroom. "Looks like somebody's been branded by the green girls." She hummed as she pulled on her work clothes.

"What are you talking about? I think I've developed some terrible skin condition," he said as he examined himself in the bathroom mirror. "Or maybe some blood sickness. Don't some blood diseases cause you to bruise easily? Like if you have leuk—"

"Oh, honey," Naomi laughed. "Your blood is just fine—excellent vintage, as a matter of fact." She turned to examine her backside in the dresser mirror. "I *do* like the way I look in this outfit." Naomi turned back to Devon. "Anyway, that's what the green girls told me—that you taste like, how did they put it?" Distractedly, she again glanced at the mirror, this time to fluff her glossy, curly hair. "Oh yeah—you have a 'rich aroma, a robust mouthfeel, and multi-textured palette of flavors.'"

Naomi walked towards the bedroom door. "In other words," she added as she exited the room, "You taste *good.*"

"The green girls?" Devon said hoarsely. "You talk to the green girls? The nymphs?" Before he could chase after her, which would have taken great effort as he was exhausted, he heard her traipse down the staircase, and then she was out the front door. She slammed it behind her.

Devon went back to bed, too tired to call into work and too confused to talk to his manager, anyway.

****

The nymphs surrounded Devon, and again breathed sweet words to him, again stroking and kissing the exposed flesh of his neck and chest. Giggling and whispering among themselves, they pulled him down to a mossy bed by a quiet, clear pool—and swarmed him, roughly latching their mouths onto him and feeding like frenzied leeches.

Flowers of pain, blossoms of ecstasy bloomed in his mind with each pull from their hungry, suckling lips. And with every draw, Devon could feel his energy drain from his body; he could feel a weight like a heavy stone pressing against his chest, pushing his last breath from his lungs. He whimpered.

The nymph closest to his face raised her head from his neck, and Devon saw—for the first time—the true face of one of his playmates. Her skin was still pale green but mottled with sickly gray splotches. Her hair was a tangle of woody vines and long grasses, her eyes metallic and as cold as the dead space between stars. And her mouth! Her lips, slickly crimson with his blood, formed a perfect round O, and as she smiled at him, she revealed teeth with tips as sharp as ice picks, as uniform as an iron fence guarding a graveyard. Wantonly, she ran her prehensile purple tongue across those teeth before lowering her head to finish her meal.

****

Naomi, home from work, called out to Devon from the foot of the staircase. She was not surprised there was no reply; she would have been surprised if there was one. Before she headed upstairs, she walked over to the thermostat and punched in a new setting on the small green screen. Humming to herself, she then trotted up to their bedroom.

The door was open, as usual; Devon never slept with it closed. *In case he needs to make a quick escape—his childhood strategy for nightmares,* she snickered to herself. *Like that would save him.*

Naomi walked over to their bed and flung the damp sheet off Devon's supine form. She held her hand above his mouth and nose—no inhalation, no exhalation. She pressed her ear to his chest. There was no rhythmic thumping to be heard—no wild horses stampeding in his chest, no languid ticking of his soul-clock.

She straightened up and looked closely at him. Even in the dim light of the bedroom, she could see he was gray and emaciated. The green girls had done their work on him, taking what they needed and then some. *Did they overdo it?* Naomi wondered. *Nah, I just wasn't prepared for the results—even though they warned me.*

But what a trade-off! Naomi rationalized to herself. *I've never looked better.*

Naomi sauntered over to her side of the bed and fluffed her cool pillow. *I've had a tiring day, and what with finding Devon like this—I'll just deal with his remains in the morning.* She undressed for an early bedtime

She slipped into bed, laid her head on her fluffy-yet-firm pillow, pulled the covers up to her chin, and closed her eyes. With a blissful sigh, she traveled to the serene, mossy grotto of her dream space, where the handsome, well-muscled satyrs danced from one green hoof to the other in lustful anticipation of her arrival—and the hungry nymphs hid in the surrounding woodland, and waited.

The End

Vampire Tutorial by Marc Shapiro

Who am I
I am
Who I am
I am the blackness
The night terror
Something to be feared
Something that feeds
Something that roams the universe
On a mission to turn the living
Into the undead
I have no conscience
No desires
Except to decimate and destroy
And stunt my never satiated hunger
There you have it
It's getting dark
Time to go
On my appointed rounds
Class dismissed

The Stolen Nun by Marge Simon

Born out of wedlock, a child of the streets,
the Sisters took me in, to nurture and instill
their divine formula to a poor mute child,
a willing novice, grateful for their care.

Oh, I believed -- devoted to the Word,
the Truth, committed my life to selflessness,
counting my rosaries on stone floors,
a paper doll in a cardboard room.
Why can't I see the light, in all this gloom?
A key turns in the lock, I hear the creak of wood --
a shadow flickers on the wall, and joins my own.
His silhouette is handsome, his deep voice, benign.
As he bends my neck to meet his lips,
he promises Eternity, and I comply.

Free Trade
by
Hal Kempka

Sam turned his Mercedes onto the gravel drive and stopped at a speaker mounted next to the driveway. The driver's side window slid down, and he pushed the "talk" button.

"Hello, this is Sam and Carla to see Harold and Brianna."

A short burst of static from the speaker followed by, "Welcome guys, we were wondering where you were."

The aqua wrought-iron gate slowly opened. Gravel crunched beneath the tires as Sam followed a tree-lined drive that sliced between the estate's spacious, verdant grounds. The path circled the fountain and garden-filled crimson roses and stopped in front of a graystone mansion.

Carla stared in awe out the car window. "Sam, these people must be freaking rich."

He parked before a driveway that led to a long, multi-doored garage. A car carrier partially loaded with luxury vehicles sat off to the side beneath an ancient, heavily branched oak tree.

"I can't believe they invited us to their home," she continued. "My stomach's been flip-flopping all morning."

Sam grabbed her hand and gave it a reassuring squeeze. "Don't worry, hon; we made it past the membership interview at the club, and I am sure we'll meet their social standards."

"Yeah, but look at this place; it's a veritable castle."

Their host Harold was the Hidden Valley country club's membership director. He'd interviewed Sam and Carla shortly after they moved into a nearby subdivision bearing the same name and applied for membership. Harold seemed cordial and gracious, and after the interview, his massive hand swallowed Sam's as he shook it.

"I think you two will fit in well as members," he'd said, and invited them to his home for an afternoon swim and BBQ.

While Sam made decent money as a bank vice-president, he had nothing in common financially with most of its members. Nearly all of them lived in an exclusive section of the already upscale neighborhood. Especially Harold, who'd built an import-export business that earned him a fortune several times over.

As they hurried up the flagstone walkway, the entryway's huge double doors swung open. Their hosts stepped out onto the terraced veranda. Harold smiled, raising his cocktail glass in a greeting while his younger-looking wife puckered her lips in a tight smile.

Brianna drew her shoulders back in a proud display of her latest cosmetic surgery success and waved. Her gossamer lounging gown strained at the seams. The women exchanged air kisses.

"Welcome to our home," Harold said. "We thought you'd never get here."

"Yes," Brianna added. "I was beginning to worry you might cancel at the last minute."

"We wouldn't do that," Sam replied. "We've been dying to see this palatial estate you call home."

Carla handed her hostess a gift bag. "Here's a little something we picked up at a little shop in Chinatown. I hope you like it."

Brianna removed the slender green-tinted wine bottle from its bag just high enough to glance at the label.

"Oh, how thoughtful; look, dear, a Chinese white wine from the Yunnan Valley."

Harold nodded his approval, and the couple led Sam and Carla inside. Their shoes tapped against the marble floor as they followed their hosts toward an oak paneled library with a wet bar. Sam and Carla sat at the bar, and Harold hurried to the other side. Brianna squeezed between them, draping her arms over their shoulders. Carla shivered as Brianna's hand occasionally swept across her breast just enough to brush the nipple, which turned visibly erect.

Sam turned from the back of the bar and set deep red goblets edged with citrus slices in front of them. Brianna hurried to the kitchen and returned with a tray of fruit, cheese, and pate-spread crackers.

"Brianna insisted on Sangria."

"Ideal for sweltering days, don't you think?" she added.

Their glasses clinked in a toast, and Harold said, "Honey, why don't you give Carla the nickel tour?"

Harold and Sam remained at the bar and watched the ladies disappear down the hall.

"Sam, I hope you won't be offended, but your wife is a hot little number; I'd bet you don't get much sleep at night with her lying next to you."

Sam's lips curled in an obligatory smile as he noted that the lecherous glint in Harold's eyes was anything but subtle.

"We have our moments," he replied. "So how is the import-export business these days, Harold, with all the trade sanctions and disease scares?"

"Doing quite well. You probably noticed the cars alongside the house. They are headed to Taiwan. We just landed them as another Pacific Rim trading partner who has been seeking something uniquely American. While I can't divulge the product at this point, we'll be fulfilling their first shipment soon. Frankly, it took a while to cut through the red tape and make all the arrangements."

Sam nodded. "That sounds quite exciting."

The ladies returned, and Brianna suggested they change into their bathing suits. They followed a winding path to the pool and changed in separate rooms in the huge cabana.

Brianna ensured their Sangria glasses never emptied once they settled into the lounge chairs outside the cabana. When their conversations turned giddy from both sun and wine, they jumped in the pool to cool off, then back out to replenish their glasses and relax in the shade. By the time the sun dipped behind the swaying palm trees, Carla and Sam looked a little tipsy.

Harold and Brianna scooted their lounge chairs a little closer to their guests, and became more touchy-feely during their conversations. At one point, Brianna rested her hand on Sam's thigh. She let it linger a moment before pulling back, letting her fingernails lightly scrape the soft skin of his inner thigh.

Brianna looked toward Harold. "Sweetheart, why don't you start the grill. I'm famished."

"I'll get right on it."

Sam stood and said, "Need any help? I'll go with you."

Brianna put a hand on his shoulder and gently settled him back onto the lounger.

"Why don't you stay here with Carla and me? I do want to know more about you two."

Harold lit the large brick barbeque and called out, "You're going to love these steaks. They're what we will be shipping overseas,"

A moment later, he disappeared down the walk toward the house. Brianna topped off the Sangria glasses and settled back in her lounge chair. The three of them continued making small talk until Sam began to slur his words.

Brianna glanced at Carla, sitting quietly and looking content and relaxed. Brianna knelt between their chairs and slid one hand along Carla's thigh. At the same time, her other hand brushed against Sam's crotch.

"Are you guys all right?" she asked. "Gosh, I hope you didn't get too much sun."

She put her arms across their shoulders and continued, "Come on, you two; let's get out of the sun. You both are burnt and looking a little pie-eyed."

She helped Carla stand and guided her into the cabana first. She then returned for Sam and helped him to his feet.

"Come on, lover," she said. "I think it is time to play inside."

Sam smiled and wobbled against her as they stumbled into the cabana. Brianna sat him at the opposite end of the couch from Carla and plopped down between them. She eyed both and leaned against Sam.

She nibbled on his ear and whispered, "Harold and I thought maybe we'd get a little more intimately acquainted with you two before dinner. Are you comfortable with that?"

Sam's head bobbed a little, and he gave her glassy-eyed grin. Carla sat in a stupor, resting against the back of the couch, her eyes fixed on the ceiling. Her breasts rose and fell with labored breathing.

Harold stepped into the cabana and pushed a covered cart toward a stainless-steel counter along the cabana wall. He glanced at the couple and smiled at Brianna

"Geez, I guess the Rohypnol in their Sangria worked really well. I hope I didn't miss anything."

"Absolutely not, my love," she cooed.

He gave Carla a peck on the cheek and stood over her from behind the couch. She gazed up at him. Her head wobbled, and her eyes looked glazed. Her lips were pressed in a sloppy pucker. He turned back to the cart and donned a rubber apron.

As he set a large platter on the counter, Brianna clapped her hands together and giggled.

"Playtime, you too," she said to the drugged couple. "Oh, goody; look, Harold is ready."

Harold chuckled and turned his attention to Carla. He stood over her, placed a canvas towel over the back of the couch, and laid her head against it. Harold patted her cheek, and she looked up at him with glazed-eyes. He swung a large wooden mallet down on her head, splattering blood and flesh, and a loud *thunk* echoed through the cabana.

Brianna giggled and took the mallet from Harold. "My turn!"

Sam sat quietly, his glazed, dilated eyes fixed on the ceiling. Brianna stepped behind him and leaned over to gaze into his eyes. She stroked his face and stepped back. She raised the mallet over Sam's head, and another splattering of blood and bits of flesh accompanied the *thunk* from her mallet.

****

Brianna and Harold lifted the couple onto a long stainless steel chef table. Sam chopped and ground the couple into steaks, chops, and roasts, and Brianna cleaned up.

He kept two steaks and wrapped the remaining meat in butcher paper. He carted the rest to the walk-in freezer to await shipment to their newest client. They now had enough of their "Premium, all-American Beef" to fill their initial order.

Later that night, Harold and Brianna sat beneath the cabana at a candlelit table. She stabbed a chunk of steak with her fork and lifted it to her lips.

"Oh, Harold, I can't believe how tender these cuts are. I do hope they catch on in the Orient, don't you?"

"Oh, I'm certain they will, my love," he replied, sipping on a glass of Merlot. "I am afraid, though; it may be profitable for only a short time. You know how free trade is in the Far East. They will create knock-offs using local sources and export them back here at a lower cost, with a larger profit margin."

The End

The Sightless Lost Souls by Matthew Wilson

I do not like the coffin
With a bat motto on the lid
I saw the man asleep in there
From the place where I had hid.

I was skipping school when it happened
When I entered this ugly place
A castle on a stinking hill
To get out of the school race.

But now the sun is low
And the coffin starts to creak
Releasing a air of dead things
A red-eyed, cloth-covered freak.

Ms. Harper would give me detention
Punishment for truancy on a roll
But I feel weird since I left there
The castle where I left my soul.

Third Degree Burn
by
Christopher Dabrowski

"Lady, you have third-degree burns," the doctor said. "Of course, you also have first and second degree burn but the third is the most extensive."

I felt my skin going numb. It is terrible! What now?

"Doctor, nothing can be done?"

"Unfortunately, your skin must be removed."

"Removed," I muttered as if in a trance.

"We will do everything that you do not suffer."

But I do not know if I can survive this. Indeed, I could not imagine how I'd make it home now.

The doctor of dermatology was silent; he did everything he could. God, all those stairs… first step … fourth, fifth, and now this.

Nobody told me to store the most corrosive acid in the world… It is my fault.

The End

While the Light Lasts by Matthew Wilson

There is nothing worse than a low set sun
Its reassuring lick of light so weak in the sky
Knowing what creatures wake when the night has won
To feast on the good that without light will die.

In the darkened valleys the song of death plays on
Growing in their duty to toast an ugly moon
To spit on heroes' stones when the light has gone
And make their spells to invoke all men's doom.

The growing night sparkles with yellow wolves' eyes
Servants to a queen of a godless land
Whose tongue knows tricks of all disguises
Whose kisses turn kings' bones to sand.

There is nothing worse than a low set sun
Resting on the stones of heroes there sleeping
Who fought and fell by a coward's gun
Smashed by vampire hands when the night comes creeping.

A Great Adventure
by
Rod Marsden

Tom Bateman met her in Bathurst during his college years. Her name was Gina. She had long, red hair and a superb figure. Was she Italian? He thought so. Yet they communicated from the start in English, and her English was excellent. He decided to learn Italian while at college, and his tutor was amazed at how well he took to the language, especially since he had never come across it in high school.

Every night since college, Gina would visit him in his sleep. He fell in love with her and she with him. Yet they would only ever get together in a dream world not of their making. She was from Milan rather than Rome. However, since growing up, he knew more about Rome than Milan. Then, if his mind had invented her, was she born and raised in Milan? Also, if he was her invention, why was he born in Sydney, Australia instead of London or New York? Someone born in Milan would surely know more about London or New York than Sydney. What's more, as he aged, so did she. If she was a phantom, she should have remained forever young, and he, for her, would have stayed the same.

Their place of mutual dreaming was a castle like the one in Disneyland. The servants were kind, and the wine provided was excellent and sweet. In the wakening world, he was a beer drinker but not when in the arms of Gina. They made love numerous times over the years, each wishing to visit the other's conscious domain in real life. Neither could afford to travel such a distance and each dreaded rejection from the other in the so-called real world.

Tom had grown up in a small town on the outskirts of Bankstown in New South Wales. It was the 1960s, a time of complete confusion regarding his rights. There was the sexual revolution created by the pill and the uprising among the young against the Vietnam War. He had long hair and saw Jesus Christ Superstar live on stage. Then there was women's liberation. It shocked him at first, and he thought of it as just another barrier thrown up by society to prevent him from experiencing happiness with the opposite sex. It was bizarre then that what he so desired began in a college situated in the middle of the country with a dream that was the start of numerous other dreams. Tom and Gina were equals in that place, and neither wanted it any other way. He neither cared to dominate nor be dominated. She understood this and agreed to a way of life that complimented each other.

In 1972, Australia pulled out of the Vietnam War, and a few years later, so did the USA. By then, the promise of Disco was done, exposed as a lie, and Tom found going to discos tedious. He went to a few then stopped, realizing they were a place to get drunk and listen to bad music. It was in the early 1980s that he was accepted to a college and there, his life improved considerably. He was lonely, and so he didn't take much stock in the first dream, and neither did Gina. He recalled dancing with her a ballroom dance and thoroughly enjoying himself, the nonsense of disco left behind. He was surprised when Gina returned to their shared subconscious state the following night. How long can this possibly go on for, he wondered. He was tempted to ask someone in the psychology department about this but was afraid an examination of this phenomenon would make it vanish forever. If it was only a dream, he wanted to keep it for as long as possible.

It was a trifle, but Gina's lips always smelled of strawberries. In spring in Australia and autumn in Milan, she wore the faintest whiff of vanilla. He remarked at this once, but all he got back from her was a smile. On one occasion, she told him he smelled of books and newspapers. While at the castle, he oft times dressed like a knight and she a maiden.

Sometime in the 1990s, Gina gave birth to a daughter. The child was born in that realm they shared. She grew up there in the company of servants and loving parents. Tom and Gina were so pleased. They called her Maria, and she developed the kind of red hair her mother had. They taught her English and Italian. Tom shared his knowledge of books as did Gina. In such a locale, Tom and Gina were excellent cooks, something most Australian men growing up in the 1960s were loathe to become. Yet here, in their castle, it was okay for a man to develop culinary skills. In the waking world, he pretended to know less than he did about cooking. In Gina and Maria's company, however, he was more himself.

In 2015, Maria left home for studies abroad. Tom and Gina were sad to see her go but understood why this had to be so. She had grown up and so had to explore more of her world. Again, there was evidence that these dreams were indeed more than a flight of fancy for either. In the real world, Tom became a government clerk, and so did Gina. It was because he once shared a home with an unscrupulous woman that Tom could never save up for a trip to Italy, even if he had the nerve to go. By the time he left the company of that terrible creature, too much time had gone by, and he had developed cancer. Around the same time, the flesh-and-blood Gina came down with pneumonia. It was a dream-like state that surprised her doctor when she called for Tom and smiled. In the year 2017, Gina passed away. The doctor thought she died alone, but Gina and Tom, knew better. She remained, however, in the place of dreams until Tom died two years later.

What then was the fate of Tom, Gina, and Maria? A world unlike any other opened for them, and both Tom and Gina were young again. Maria visited them in their new castle from time to time, and they remained happy with one another.

The End

Festival of Dead Gods by Matthew Wilson

I wanted to go to the music festival
sneaking out when mum's bedroom light went off
careful to miss the zipping cars by Starlight
but I had sold all my comics for the tickets.

The piggish man at the gate asked no questions
as I pushed through the axe-wielding crowd
where rock gods played his interesting guitar
using his slaves' howls as background music.

For fireworks they torched the crosses
throwing petrol on men nailed there
cutting their lyrics in their flesh
using their backs for the second chorus.

In that pit of spikes, we moshed all night
drinking the free blood goblets they passed around
till the whistle interrupted the banshee
and the human lynch mob bust through the gates.

I still don't know how I dodged their gunfire
sneaking back through the excited traffic to home
beating Mom from her own midnight adventures
heading to my coffin before the deadly dawn.

Haiku Two by Denny E. Marshall

almost nobody
willing to work the nightshift
except vampires

French Maid by Marge Simon

Michelle, my Michelle
so fetching in your demi-apron,
all aflutter, pouring his tea,
wiping crumbs from his lips
with your dainty handkerchief,
singing him to sleep with
"Frere Jacque", knowing
he doesn't understand
it is a morning song.

Michelle, my Michelle
can't you hear his silver bell?
You're one of us now,
time to serve your master --
wheel him in, we're drooling
for a taste of his noble blood.

Stairs to Heaven
by
Christopher T. Dabrowski

At the top of the highest stairs, tragedy happened. A podge staggered and screaming, he fell backward together with others. An older woman tumbled into an old man, scalping his bald spot with her denture. Blinded by blood flooding his eyes, the wounded man waved his walking stick, jabbing it into the eye of a young woman. Her name is Basia. Basia was well-endowed. As she fell into Adaś, the man behind her, she suffocated him with her breasts. Adaś fell into a group of photographers insanely flashing their cameras.

Before they realized what had happened, they were a mess of broken bones. Bloody pulp covered everything downstairs. The untouched stairs worked on taking more victims to the top. These were the stairs to heaven – they took everyone on their last journey.

The End

I See Red by Marc Shapiro

I don't always see well at night
But I know where the blood is
I can tell when a vein is full
And fat
And ripe for my fangs
I can spot a source a mile away
They come in all shapes and sizes
Vulnerable
Hopeful
Looking for something
Anything
In the night
At that moment I strike
Drink my fill
And continue to live
Forever
And in plain sight

Yōkai
by
Rajeev Bhargava

"I was surrounded by monsters of all shapes and sizes; trapped inside a secret room, thinking myself safely hidden away and free from danger; but alas they discovered me and so ... I had no option but to raise my samurai sword, to avoid being eaten alive, and committed hara-kiri." ~*Death Call: A Samurai Ghost's Recollection of his Death*

Japan, Tokyo, and inside their parents' exotic and simple, beautifully decorated home, a husband and wife in their mid-fifties were sitting on the floor, barefooted and in light spring clothing. It was midday, and they were trying to stay cool in the shade during an intense heat wave, gazing through the sliding open door facing their courtyard at the beautiful and elegant pink-leaved tree. That was when Yudhishtira spoke.

"You know, Yoshimi, I still remember planting that tree with Mum when I had just turned nine. It seems like only yesterday; how time flies. Can you remember what you were doing at the time?"

There was no response. He turned to her and gave her a gentle prod. She seemed lost in thought, staring at the tree, and then softly sang out, stamping her bare feet on the floor with full force:

> *"For the dead won't wake until it starts to get late, oh Yōkai! Oh Yōkai!*
> *For the dead won't wait until it starts to get late, oh Yōkai! Oh Yōkai!*
> *For the dead won't wait until it starts to get late, oh Yōkai! Oh Yōkai!*

He looked at her, bewildered, and then gave her a prod.

"Yoshimi. Why are you acting so strangely?" asked Yudhishtira.

She turned towards him, and her head morphed into that of a turtle with golden-yellow eyes, then swiftly back to normal, after which an ecstatic smile formed across her face.

"Oh, Yudhi," she said, waving her beautiful Japanese fan, "I just remembered. I'd prepared some sushi for you in the kitchen. Don't worry. I've prepared it as a vegan dish the way you like. It's small balls of cold rice garnished with vegetables. Now you wait right here, and I'll serve it to you. *Sayonara!*" She giggled, took a bow, and waved her hands.

Before he could react, she rose to her feet and left for the kitchen. He rubbed his eyes.

"Did I *really* see what I just did? No, it must be my imagination, most likely a hallucination caused by this heat."

He shrugged, then called out, "While you're there, my love, could you please bring me some beer? Thank you, Yosh." He grinned and lay on the floor with a pillow.

Before long, she returned, holding a tray with the food and drink displayed. She smiled and knelt, carefully placing it on a low table. Yudhi looked at her again and caressed her hair.

"What is it, Yudhi? Your eyes are filling with tears. Is everything all right?"

"I'm sorry, Yoshima. I was thinking of my parents." He rose to his feet and reached out for a family album from a cabinet. He opened it and gazed at their wedding photos. He then sat beside her, and they looked through it.

"It's really amazing and so romantic how Mum and Dad met," he said.

"Yes, when Dad was a single bachelor in Japan, Tokyo, he was sent on an official tour to India, New Delhi, where he met Mum," responded Yoshimi.

"Hmm, and that is when they met, and it was love at first sight." He looked at her and smiled. "Hey, you never could pronounce my full name, Yudhishtira, but it's all right. I love it when you call me Yudhi." They both smiled and hugged, then ate their lunch. Just then, Yoshimi faded into thin air and reappeared in a few seconds.

"Everything all right, Yudhi? You look as if you've seen a ghost!" She giggled and poked him.

He jumped and trembled.

"Oh, Yudhi, you're shaking."

"I think I'll go and take a bath."

Yudhi stood up and made his way to the bathroom. Along the way, he joined his hands in prayer at a statue of Lord Buddha.

"Oh Buddha, please give me the strength to remain positive and only do good karma."

As he turned around the corner, he looked up on the wall at a mounted samurai sword, which had once been owned by one of his great ancestors and fell into his father's hands.

"I always feel uneasy looking at you," he said to the sword, then retreated to the bathroom.

Once Yudhi was naked, he dipped his toes in the tub and then entered slowly. The water was warm. He felt so relaxed that his eyes closed. He smiled.

"Aah, this is pure heaven. No devils in here."

Suddenly, the bathroom door slid open, and a ghostly apparition appeared in front of him, letting out a loud shriek.

Yudhishtra's eyes burst open, and he found himself in a tub full of blood and torn limbs. A decapitated head bobbed in the tub along his left arm.

Screaming, he jumped out of the tub and noticed the figure blocking the door.

"The devil! Aaaaahhhhh!"

"I am Shikako, the evil and naughty twin sister of your beloved wife, Yoshimi … and I am going to haunt you to death," she called out in a hollow and eerie voice. Her laughter echoed across the walls.

He closed his eyes and ran through the apparition into the main room, slipping, still naked on the floor.

"Is everything all right, Yudhi? Oh! You're naked." She giggled and rushed to get a towel, then stopped. Her head changed into the same turtle that called out:

"Or maybe you prefer to stay as you are." Then it changed back to her again.

"You … you're shapeshifting and continually possessing animal features," Yudhi cried. "Just like a Kappa. Yes, and that horror in the bathroom must be *Mononoke* spirit. It said it was your twin sister called Shikako. But how is that possible? Oh, great Buddha, please save my sanity."

"I'm no expert in Japanese mythology, but even a simple girl like me knows they are properly referred to as Yōkai!" She rubbed his hair and then added,

"Now, I will get you some rice and green tea for your meal, Yosh, and we can talk it over then, hmm?" He opened his mouth to reply, but she had left for the kitchen, giggling.

She had no sooner left when blood dripped from around the ceiling borders. He stood up, alarmed, and called out,

"Yoshimi!" He rushed to the kitchen to find it empty and looked around frantically.

"Hey, handsome. Look above you!" He turned his head and saw Shikako glued to the ceiling in a see-through flesh-coloured robe. Her mouth opened wide and she vomited a yellow froth that soaked through his naked body.

"Yudhi! Ready for your meal?" It was Yoshimi. Just then, everything turned back to normal, and he found himself in a blue robe and seated cross-legged on the floor. She giggled.

"Decided to wear some clothes after all? I quite preferred you without them." She winked, laid out the food on the table at floor level, and joined him. He stared at her, wide-eyed, and nodded.

"Yoshima, do you think I'm normal?"

"Of course. Why do you say such things? Is something troubling you?"

He looked up at the ceiling and pointed.

"While you were in the kitchen, I noticed blood all around our ceiling and walls, and … Shikako was stuck up there."

"Stop!! I don't expect such talk from you. I will forget what I heard and demand that you act normal and eat your meal this instant."

He looked at her and caressed her hair then they ate their meal.

That night, Shikako appeared again, lying beside him on the floor. He awoke in a sweat, and she then vanished into thin air.

"I've made up my mind. There's only one thing left for me to do. I must go to Dad's secret basement and look for his journals on exorcism. There will be a clue there. Please forgive me." He tiptoed barefoot and peered across the floor at the other side of the bedroom, where his wife Yoshima lay in a deep sleep.

"Good. I think I'll go down to the basement now."

Once there, he nodded and brushed his hands through his hair.

"Damn. There's a heavy lock across it, and it's corroded. I'll need to break that chain with something … but what?" He thought for a while and then:

"Of course! Dad's samurai sword!" He tiptoed to the wall, carefully removed it with the greatest care, then returned to the lock. After this, with one swift strike, he struck it against the chain, which shattered into tiny pieces. He smiled, then bent down to pull open the door.

A flight of steps ran down, blanketed in total darkness.

"I need a light. Wait, there's a lantern on a hook against the first step. Dad always was a great organiser."

As he made his way down with the lantern, he observed that each step he walked on became a multitude of bright colours. First red, then blue, then green, then yellow, then orange, which illuminated the room and made it easier for him to soon reach the massive room where there was a desk. On the desk lay a large red and yellow book.

Yudhi placed the lantern on the desk, then read the book cover.

"My Journal of the Shoku Nihongi history (c. 797) and My Encounters with A Hoshi Exorcist officiating burial ceremonies for Emperor Konin (781) and Emperor Kanmu (806): by Toshiro Raiki."

"What a long title. Typical of Dad!"

He turned the first page which he read out softly:

"'I have summoned this estranged exorcist at the burial ceremony of my wife, Parineeti.' No! It can't be possible; that's Mum! It means … he was trying to bring her back to life. But how can this be possible? Even this creepy unnamed exorcist lived so many centuries ago. He can't be a human, surely."

He flicked the pages forwards and saw some magic spells.

"Mantra to summon the dead."

Just then, there was a loud thud. It was the basement door. Somehow it had been shut. He also heard moving chains and a bolt securing the door. He was trapped inside.

Just then, Shikako appeared, and beside her stood none other than his own wife, Yoshima, holding a plate of rice.

"Yosh! That's the girl I've been telling you about. Her name is Shikako!"

Yoshima turned to Shikako. A moment's silence and then, both burst into a fit of manic laughter. After which, they closed in on him. Shikako gazed at the book. Her eyes turned bright red, and flames of fire burst out and burnt the book to cinders. She then turned to their victim.

"You walked right into our trap. You even allowed us to destroy that book. Now, it is time for you to die." She turned to Yoshima.

"I hope you're not a vegan, my sweet sister?"

Yoshika giggled and morphed, changing into a reptilian animal. She hissed. Drool came out of her mouth, dripping onto the floor.

"Let's not wait any longer. I'm soooo hungry! Ssssss!"

"A feast of human-vegan sushi!" cried Shikako.

Shikako reached forwards, pulled, and ripped out his tongue, after which they spat out venom simultaneously. Finally, they tore him apart slowly, fingers first, toes, then all body parts which they relished and enjoyed.

Before long, all that remained was a heap of bones they used as ornaments to decorate themselves and display as a warning *never* to challenge their kind, known as the Yōkai.

The End.

About the Contributors

Linda Barrett:

Ms. Barrett has been writing all her life. She wrote her first book at the age of eight. It's still in the McKinley Elementary school library. She was published in the *Huntingdon Junior Library* literary magazine by age thirteen. She's won three awards with the Montgomery County Community College Writer's contest. "Mr. Cat's Revenge" won third place in the 2014 MCCC contest. Ms. Barrett lives with her 84 years young mother in Abington in the same house for 50 years."

Rajeev Bhargava:

Rajeev lives in Harrow with his parents and five Chihuahuas. He has been writing since the age of twelve but had his first work published in 1990. Since then, he's been writing stories, poems and articles for the small press as well as mainstream. His ambition is to be a freelance writer.

Alexis Child:

Alexis Child hails from Toronto, Canada, home to dreams and nightmares. She worked at a Call Crisis Center befriending demons of the mind that roam freely amongst her writings. Alexis once lived with a Calico-cat child sleuthing all that went bump in the night and is haunted by the memory of her cat. She is currently working on her second poetry collection and starving in the garret with her muse. A starving child is a frightful sight. A starving vampire is even worse. Please donate nonperishable food items and B-negative blood (and make it a double!).

Alexis Child's fiction has been featured in *Danse Macabre, Schlock, Screams of Terror*, and UK's *Dark of Night Magazine*. Her poetry has been featured in numerous online and print publications, including *Aphelion, Black Petals, Blood Moon Rising Magazine, The Horror Zine, The Sirens Call*, and elsewhere. Her first collection of poetry, *Devil in the Clock*, a dark and sinister slice of the macabre, is now available on Amazon.

Visit her website: http://www.angelfire.com/poetry/alexischild/; Alexis's YouTube Channel: https://www.youtube.com/channel/UCg6S5u4yX73kA1ZWGnKaEBA/videos

Christopher T. Dabrowski:

Christopher has had numerous books published in the USA and Poland. His USA works include: *Anomaly* and *Escape*, both published by the Royal Hawaiian Press. Books published in Poland include *Anima Vilis* (Initium), *Grobbing* (Novae Res), *Deathbirth and other Stories* (Agharta & Amoryka), *Orgazmokalipsa* (Alternatywne publishing house), *Anomalia* (Forma publishing house), and *Ucieczka* (2017 - Dom Horroru publishing house). Monika Olasek provided the English translation for his *Night to Dawn* stories.

Sandy DeLuca:

Sandy has written five novels; *Settling in Nazareth* (she painted the cover art), *Descent, Manhattan Grimoire, From Ashes,* and *Requiem for the Dead*. Her poetry chapbook, *Burial Plot in Sagittarius* (also created cover art and illustrations), was nominated for the BRAM STOKER award in 2001. Her art has been exhibited in galleries, hair salons, book stores and online venues. She has also painted covers and contributed interior illustrations for various numerous small press venues.

Chris Friend:

Chris has published his art in small press horror magazines for nearly 25 years. His surreal horror images have been featured in *Stygian Articles, Realm of the Vampire, Deathrealm, Black Petals,* and *Space and Time*. He draws his inspiration from Harry Clarke, H. R. Giger, and the horror comics of the 70s such as the Tomb of Dracula her and the Hammer Studios Frankenstein films. Chris friend can be reached at Mars_art_13@yahoo.com. Chris friend can be reached at Mars_art_13@yahoo.com.

To sample his illustrations, go to http://chris.michaelherring.net and http://www.moonlit-path.com/art-2-13-06.htm.

Ken Goldman:

Ken Goldman, former Philadelphia teacher of English and Film Studies, is an Active member of the Horror Writers Association. He has homes on the Main Line in Pennsylvania and at the Jersey shore. His stories have appeared in over 960 independent press publications in the U.S., Canada, the UK, and Australia with over twenty due for publication in 2021. Since 1993, Ken's tales have received seven honorable mentions in *The Year's Best Fantasy & Horror*. He has written six books: three anthologies of short stories, *You Had Me at ARRGH!!* (Sam's Dot Publishers), *Donny Doesn't Live Here Anymore* (A/A Productions) and *Star-Crossed* (Vampires 2); and a novella, *Desiree*, (Damnation Books). His first novel *Of a Feather* (Horrific Tales Publishing) was released in January 2014. *Sinkhole*, his second novel, was published by Bloodshot Books August 2017.

Todd Hanks:

The creative writing of Todd Hanks has been seen in publications such as Asimov's Science Fiction Magazine and the Kansas City Star newspaper.

Tom Johnson:

Tom, a Vietnam veteran with twenty years in the military police (L.E.), has enjoyed literary success as a science fiction novelist with his action adventures in the Jurassic Period of Earth's predawn. He has created short story SF characters like Captain Danger of the *Space Rangers* and the galactic master thief, *The Forever Man* as futuristic space opera adventure. His many costumed crime fighters include two of his own creations, such as *The Black Ghost* and *The Masked Avenger*, as well as a western masked hero of the plains called *The Nightwind*. He has upcoming stories of *Ki-Gor the Jungle Lord*, and Greek heroes like Hercules and Atalanta. For the latest information on Tom and his writing, check out his websites:

http://www15.brinkster.com/jur1/index.html
www.geocities.com/fadingshadows1/index.html.

Hal Kempka:

Hal's stories have been published in numerous magazines and ezines including *Night to Dawn, Blood Moon Rising, Black Petals, Inner Sins, Sanitarium, Yellow Mama,* and *Microhorror*. His horror short fiction anthologies, *Blue Plate Special* and *Discarded Treasures,* are currently available on Amazon Kindle, Barnes and Noble, and Smashwords, among others. *Discarded Treasures* is available in both paperback and e-book. Other anthologies including his stories are Pill Hill Press: *Zombie Art Inspired Short Stories, Blood Bound Books: Seasons in the Abyss*, and Post Mortem Press: *Shadowplay*.

Hillary Lyon:

With an MA in English Literature from SMU, Hillary Lyon founded and for 20 years served as senior editor for the independent poetry publisher, Subsynchronous Press. Her speculative, horror, and sci-fi stories have appeared in numerous print and online publications. She's also an illustrator for horror/sci-fi, and pulp fiction sites. And she loves to hand-paint furniture and accessories.

Rod Marsden:

Rod Marsden hails from Sydney, Australia. He has three degrees related to writing and history. His stories have been published in Australia, England, Russia, the USA and now Canada. He has work in the American anthology *Cats Do it Better,* the American steam punkanthology *Break Time* and in the Canadian anthology *Morbid Metamorphosis*. Many of his short stories have been published in *Night to Dawn* magazine. His books include *Undead Reb Down Under and Other Vampire Stories, Disco Evil: Dead Man's Stand, Ghost Dance,* and *Desk Job* (his salute to Lewis Carroll). *Cold Water Conscience* is his venture into Crime/Horror. His short play, *Zombie Vision*, was well received at Cronulla Arts Theatre. His play *Hyde and Seek* was even better received. Rod has a fondness for Cronulla and the Wollongong area but an abiding love for the more northern Clarence River region of his home state of New South Wales.

Denny E. Marshall:

Denny E. Marshall has had art, poetry, and fiction published. Some recent credits include interior art in *Midnight Echo #14* Dec. 2019, cover art for *Society Of Misfit Stories* Feb. 2020, and poetry in *Space & Time Magazine #134* Fall 2019. This year his website is celebrating 20 years on the web. Also in 2020 his artwork is for sale for the first time. It is available on Zazzle as posters coffee cups, puzzles, mouse pads, etc. The link is on his website. (Click on top left drawing.) See more at www.dennymarshall.com.

Elizabeth Hattie Pierce-Collins:

Elizabeth first learned art and drawing from her mother. From there, she was self-taught until she was able to attend art school. She loves drawing the human figure and never stops studying the human body in motion. Her illustrations have appeared in *Night to Dawn* magazine and *The Spider's Web* (a novel). These have drawn positive attention from the readers. Elizabeth hopes to appear in more magazines and books in the future. For more information, contact Elizabeth at wackyursalinan45@aol.com.

Katherine Quevedo:

Katherine Quevedo was born and raised just outside of Portland, Oregon, where she works as an analyst and lives with her husband and two sons. Her fiction has appeared or is forthcoming in *Nightmare Magazine*, Flame Tree Publishing's *Christmas Gothic, Triangulation: Habitats, Frost Zone Zine*, and elsewhere. "Hell-ium Balloon" first appeared in *Last Girls Club*. When she isn't writing, she enjoys watching movies, singing, playing old-school video games, belly dancing, and making spreadsheets. Find her at www.katherinequevedo.com.

Anna Rose:

Anna Rose is a writer, a smart-ass, and takes no prisoners. She is currently working on several projects, because she's never quite been able to figure out how to focus on just one thing. Welcome to the world of neurodivergence. Her favorite subjects to write about are the Devil, the supernatural, and other tales of the weird. The rest is subject to change without notice.

Marc Shapiro:

Marc has been a busy beaver. His story *Let Me Take You Down* was printed in book form in the Short Sharp Shocks imprint of Demain Publishing on December 31. Upcoming from Demain is his debut poetry collection *Existential Jibber Jabber*. Already out: his unauthorized biography of Keanu Reeves entitled *Keanu Reeves Excellent Adventure* (Riverdale Avenue Books) and the shortest story he's ever written, four sentences under 100 words, on the website Warp 10 Lit. Marc Shapiro has a very patient and understanding wife.

Marge Simon:

Marge Simon's works appear in publications such as DailySF Magazine, Pedestal, Dreams& Nightmares. She edits a column for the HWA Newsletter, "Blood & Spades: Poets of the Dark Side," and serves as Chair of the Board of Trustees. She won the Strange Horizons Readers Choice Award, 2010, and the SFPA's Dwarf Stars Award, 2012. She has won three Bram Stoker Awards ® for Superior Work in Poetry, two first place Rhysling Awards and the Grand Master Award from the SF Poetry Association, 2015. In addition to her poetry, she has published two prose collections: *Christina's World*, Sam's Dot Publications, 2008 and *Like Birds in the Rain*, Sam's Dot, 2007. Her poems appear in *Qualia Nous* (Written Backwards), *The Dark Phantastique* (Jasunni Productions), Spectral Realms anthologies by S.T. Joshi, and more poems will appear in *Chiral Mad 3* and *Scary Out There*, a HWA/ Simon & Schuster Y/A collection, 2015. www.margesimon.com

Lonnie D. Weems:

Every school has one: "the kid who can draw." Lonnie spent his youth being that kid. When he wasn't drawing, Lonnie could generally be found in front of the TV repeatedly watching every horror and science fiction movie or show that popped up. His favorites tend toward the Gothic: Universal, Hammer and Mario Bava films. Following a decade of military service and still more years of raising a family, Lonnie has decided to unleash "the kid who can draw" again.

Matthew Wilson:

　　Matthew Wilson has had over 150 appearances in such places as *Horror Zine, Star*Line, Spellbound, Illumen, Apokrupha Press, Gaslight Press, Sorcerers Signal* and many more. He is currently editing his first novel and can be contacted on twitter @matthew94544267.

Lee Clark Zumpe:

　　Lee Clark Zumpe has been writing and publishing horror, dark fantasy and speculative fiction since the late 1990s. His short stories and poetry have appeared in a variety of publications such as *Weird Tales, Space and Time* and *Dark Wisdom;* and in anthologies such as *Dark Horizons, Best New Zombie Tales Vol. 3, Dread Shadows in Paradise, Heroes of Red Hook* and *World War Cthulhu.* His work has earned several honorable mentions in *The Year's Best Fantasy and Horror* collections.

　　An entertainment columnist with Tampa Bay Newspapers, Lee has penned hundreds of film, theater and book reviews and has interviewed novelists as well as music industry icons such as Paddy Moloney of The Chieftains and Alan Parsons. His work for TBN has been recognized repeatedly by the Florida Press Association, including a first-place award for criticism in the 2013 Better Weekly Newspaper Contest.